Readers can't get enough of

DARK LORD
*THE EARLY YEARS

★ "[An] awe-inspiring episode. The threat in the author's blurb to consign wrongheaded reviewers to the Slave Pits of Never-Ending Toil are entirely superfluous, oh yes, for this humble lickspittle." —*Booklist* (starred review)

"Perfect deadpan humor. . . . This is wickedly funny, brilliantly told stuff, and you'll never have more fun cheering for evil." —Boing Boing

"The sarcastic humor will resonate with young teens and remind them of Gru from *Despicable Me*." —*VOYA*

"Fun in many ways." —*Kirkus Reviews*

"This delightful book will hook even a reluctant reader or two." —*SLJ*

BOOKS BY JAMIE THOMSON

Dark Lord: The Early Years
Dark Lord: School's Out

DARK LORD

*THE EARLY YEARS

~~JAMIE THOMSON~~
DIRK LLOYD

WALKER BOOKS FOR YOUNG READERS
AN IMPRINT OF BLOOMSBURY
NEW YORK   LONDON   NEW DELHI   SYDNEY

First published in Great Britain in 2011 by Orchard Books, a division of
Hachette Children's Books, a Hachette UK company
Published in the United States of America in October 2012 by
Walker Books for Young Readers, an imprint of Bloomsbury Publishing, Inc.
Paperback edition published in January 2014
www.bloomsbury.com

For information about permission to reproduce selections from this book, write to
Permissions, Walker BFYR, 1385 Broadway, New York, New York 10018
Bloomsbury books may be purchased for business or promotional use. For information
on bulk purchases please contact Macmillan Corporate and Premium Sales Department at
specialmarkets@macmillan.com

The Library of Congress has cataloged the hardcover edition as follows:
Thomson, Jamie.
[Dark Lord, the teenage years]
Dark Lord, the early years / by Jamie Thomson.
p.   cm.
Summary: Evil Dark Lord tries to recover his dignity, his power, and his lands when
an arch-foe transports him to a small town, into the body of a thirteen-year-old boy.
ISBN 978-0-8027-2849-4 (hardcover)
[1. Identity—Fiction. 2. Magic—Fiction. 3. Fantasy. 4. Humorous stories.] I. Title.
PZ7.T3747Dar 2012   [Fic]—dc23   2012007152

ISBN 978-0-8027-3541-6 (paperback)

Book design by Regina Flath and Yelena Safronova
Printed and bound in the U.S.A. by Thomson-Shore Inc., Dexter, Michigan
2 4 6 8 10 9 7 5 3 1

All papers used by Bloomsbury Publishing, Inc., are natural, recyclable products
made from wood grown in well-managed forests. The manufacturing processes
conform to the environmental regulations of the country of origin.

I dedicate this book to the greatest person I have ever known—to wit, myself: Dirk Lloyd

contents

Part Five: Separation

Epilogue:
Sooz in the Darklands   285

DARK LORD

*THE EARLY YEARS

Part One: Arrival

The FALL

"Aaaaaaaaaaaarrrrrrrrrrrrggggggggggghhhhhhh!"

His fall seemed to go on forever. It felt like bits of him were being stripped away, as if he was changing into something else as he fell. After a long time his cries of rage and fear faded and he sank into a kind of sleep, all sensation lost, falling silently in an immense void of nothingness for what seemed like an eternity. Then, suddenly . . .

Ka-runch!!!!

Pain, so much pain . . . Then it faded away, and he took in a great shuddering gulp of air. He coughed and spat out a glob of black mucus. He watched as the mucus formed a small puddle of shiny black oil. He lay for a while, just breathing.

The ground felt like hard gravel. He could barely move. He couldn't think properly and he felt weak and listless. The sky above was blue, painfully blue. He hated blue skies and sunlight.

He needed help. He called out for his lieutenant, Dread Gargon, Hewer of Limbs, but his voice caught in his throat. He tried again.

"Gaa . . . Gargon, to me!" he tried to bellow in his most commanding tones, but it only came out as a little squeak, high-pitched and boyish. Where was the dark, imperious voice that sent forth his Legions of Dread to bloody war and pitiless plunder?

He tried once more, but again it came out as a high-pitched trill. He groaned and tried raising his head, but couldn't. He wondered whether his Helm of the Hosts of Hades had slipped off again—if it wasn't balanced just right it could catch his neck in an uncomfortable pinch.

He reached up, but there was no helm at all. He couldn't feel any horns either, or knobby ridges of bone, only what seemed like a brown mop of hair on a rather small head. And his teeth! They didn't feel right either—no tusks or yellowed fangs to inspire terror and dread. Instead his head felt like a little human head, just like the ones he usually kept impaled on those iron spikes over the Gates of Doom, or the ones that Gargon wore hanging from his belt.

What was going on and where was Gargon?

There was something else as well. Too much harsh sunlight usually fried his undead flesh like an egg in a pan, but he couldn't feel the usual sunfire burns. Not only that, the sky actually seemed rather beautiful.

White clouds drifted serenely across the bright blue canopy of the heavens, and birds sang songs of joy in nearby trees. The sun warmed him nicely, and a feeling of . . . hmmm, let's see now, something he hadn't felt in eons, a sense of . . . *peace* came over him! Yes, that was it. A sense of peace. How could that be? He'd spent years trying to perfect a spell to cover the sky in the Black Vapors of Gloom but now the bright blueness didn't seem to bother him.

A wash of pain came over him again. That's better, he thought. He didn't want to feel a sense of peace. It just wasn't the sort of thing he should be feeling. After all, he had his reputation to consider . . .

With a great effort he was able to turn his head a little and take his eyes off the sky. He saw a low building of dull gray stone on his left, squat and unsightly. Excellent. At least someone was making ugly stuff around here. Maybe it was of Orcish design. You could always rely on Orcs to make ugly stuff.

He saw some kind of banner flying over the building. Runes were written on it, in a strange language. To his surprise he realized he could read them. SAVEMART SUPERMARKET, it said. A market. That didn't sound Orcish. Orcs tended to prefer pillaging to shopping. And Savemart—was he the local overlord, perhaps? Lord Savemart, Smiter of Foes, the Pitiless One? Something about it didn't sound right.

He looked the other way. What he saw was even stranger to his eyes. Several rows of oddly shaped metal boxes gleamed in the sunlight. They were all kinds of different colors, and glass plates had been set into their sides. They rested on four wheels, thickly encrusted with some kind of black resin that looked like the hard-set mucus of the Giant Spiderbeasts of Skorpulos. One of the boxes suddenly shuddered to life, rattling away with a terrible noise like the coughing shriek of the dragon before it discharged its fiery breath.

He tried to bend the box to his will. If it was a thing of evil, it should instinctively follow his command. "Beast of Steel and Mucus—I command you in the name of the Dark Lord and by the Power of the Nine Netherworlds!"

But his voice came out as a querulous squeak. The metal box moved away as if he hadn't even spoken. Then he noticed what looked like a human woman inside the box, peering out through the glass panels. Of course! It was some kind of horseless chariot, driven no doubt by magic. The woman must be a potent witch indeed to command such a thing. The wizardry of mortals was getting sophisticated and powerful. He'd have to watch them more closely.

Then he heard a voice—another human by the sound of it—shouting, "Hey, are you all right, son?"

His interest sharpened. A son's lifeblood would

help to perk him up. He looked around for the boy the human was talking about but couldn't see any children. Instead he saw two men running toward him, both dressed in curious dark-blue uniforms. They looked like a typical pair of ignorant, dumb-as-dormice human soldiers; though their uniforms didn't look very useful for war, and their caps wouldn't stop a sword or an ax, let alone a Goblin pike or an Orc arrow.

He tried to laugh maniacally and tell the humans to flee for their lives or be utterly destroyed, but all that came out was a cough. He tried unsuccessfully to sit up. He was still too weak. The human soldiers stood over him.

Surely his life couldn't end like this, lying helpless, waiting to be killed by a couple of ordinary humans? But then an odd thing happened. One of the warriors bent down and cradled his head. Was he trying to help him?

"Better call an ambulance, Phil."

The man who had spoken leaned closer, looking him over. (Stupid human. Didn't the fool realize who he was dealing with?) Immediately he tried ripping the man's throat out with his iron-taloned Gauntlets of Ineluctable Destruction, but it was no good—he just didn't have the strength. Then he noticed he wasn't wearing any gauntlets, or even gloves. His hands were pink, pallid, and pudgy, with neat little white nails, like those of a wretched little human boy! You couldn't even rip out the throat of a rat with those hands, let alone a fully grown human warrior. He groaned in despair.

The other human whispered something into a little black box attached to the front of his uniform. The black box crackled and spoke back to him! It must have some kind of sprite or minor demon bound into it to do his bidding. That would have taken powerful sorcery. Perhaps they were more than just ordinary human soldiers. Or more likely they served a mighty human wizard king, maybe even the White Wizard himself, Hasdruban the Pure. Hmm, he'd have to bear that in mind.

The human called Phil said, "Okay, ambulance called in."

The other one said, "Don't worry, son, we're police officers. I'm Officer Smith. You can call me John. That's Officer Phil Johnson. The ambulance will be here soon. Take it easy. Best not to move until we know what's wrong with you."

Well, the police officer was right—there certainly was something wrong with him. He couldn't move properly even if he wanted to and his body felt smaller than it should.

The one called Phil said, "Have you got a cell phone, son? We should call your mom or dad."

He wants me to sell a fone? But what's a fone? What was this cretinous manling talking about? And what curious names! Jon? Jon the Smith. Had he made the strange black box in his blacksmithy? And Fill. Fill the land with their dead? Fill your heart with hate, perhaps? What did it mean?

Either way, it was time they knew who was master here. He tried blasting them with the spell of Agonizing Obedience, but he couldn't shape his hands properly or put the right syllables together. It was as if his tongue wouldn't obey him. He couldn't believe what was happening. Where were his powers of domination and destruction?

"What's that he's wrapped in?" said Officer Smith.

"I dunno," said Officer Johnson. "It looks like some kind of oversized blanket. Black blanket though— that's odd. All those weird red, shiny patterns all over it as well. Looks foreign."

"My nephew's got something like it. I think it's from some fantasy game or film with wizards and dragons and stuff," said Officer Smith.

His robes! So he was still wearing his Cloak of Endless Night. Excellent. They didn't realize those "weird red, shiny patterns" were Blood Glyphs of Power. Each glyph was a mighty spell. Now he had them!

He managed to crane his neck, focusing on one of the glyphs. It was the Glyph of Domination. All he had

Puny humans! Oh, if only I had my
Gauntlets of Ineluctable Destruction!

to do was read it out loud and all the creatures within a hundred-mile radius would be his to command. But he couldn't read it. It didn't make any sense; it seemed completely meaningless. Why could he not understand the glyphs? After all, he had created them! Had they been stripped of their power somehow? What was happening?

The humans were still blathering on, blissfully unaware of his attempts to destroy them.

"Does he speak English? What's your name, kid?" asked Officer Johnson.

The kid, for that's what he looked like, thought for a moment. He couldn't remember his name. No matter how hard he tried, he just couldn't. But he could remember what he was, and his primary title.

"Daa . . . (cough, cough). I am the Dark Lord," he said. To his horror, he realized his voice really did sound like some kind of do-gooding Elf woman or a human boy-child!

"Dirk? Did you say Dirk?"

"No! No! Dark! Dark Lord." But his voice came out wrong, weak and raspy and even more boyish than before.

"Dirk, eh? Dirk Lloyd? Where are your mom and dad, Dirk? Have you been hit by a car? Are you lost, son?"

"Mom and dad?" he sputtered, outraged. "I don't have parents, you curs—I am the Incarnation of Evil!

The World Burner! The Dark One, to name but a few of my titles! I'm not someone's little boy, you fools!"

"These computer games. It's an obsession at their age," said Officer Johnson. "Do you know your address, Dirk? Can you tell us what happened?"

"Not Dirk, *Dark*! My address is the Iron Tower of Despair, beyond the Plains of Desolation, in the Darklands. And I haven't been 'hit by a car' . . . Er, what is a car?"

The two police officers exchanged bemused glances.

"How come he doesn't know what a car is?" Officer Smith asked. "Unless maybe he was hit by one, and now he's suffering from some kind of posttraumatic stress—he's blocked out the memory of it all and taken on the personality of a video game character as a way to deal with it. Who knows?"

"Yup, looks like this one's for social services, that's for sure! I think they'll need a child psychologist as well," replied Johnson.

As he said this, he pointed a finger at his own temple and moved it around in a circle, as if he were drilling into his skull.

Officer Smith nodded, but gestured with his eyes at "Dirk."

"Not in front of the kid," he hissed.

"What? Oh, yeah, sorry, sorry . . . Ah, here comes the ambulance."

THE CHARIOT OF DEATH

A big, white square metal box thing came hurtling toward them, hardened mucus wheels of the Spider-beasts of Skorpulos spinning furiously. On top, some kind of elemental Spirit of Air had been magically bound into a glass container, and it was flashing bright red and shrieking in agony. Its cries of pain were so loud it hurt his ears. They were cruel, these humans, he thought. Even he, a Dark Lord, wouldn't torture an elemental like that, unless he really had to, or if it had wronged him in some way. It just wasn't an efficient way of doing things.

The metal box pulled up beside them. The air elemental ceased its agonized shrieking at last. Something like jaws opened at the back. Then a man and a woman dressed in dark-green clothes came out, pulling a gurney between them.

Ah! he thought to himself. They are doors, not jaws. Of course! And the humans must be from some other branch of the humans' armed forces, but they looked even less useful as soldiers than the men dressed in blue.

"What's your name, young man?" said the woman breezily, obviously trying to give off an air of confident assurance.

Aha, he thought, perhaps she has an idea of who I am and is trying to cover up her fear.

Then one of the police officers said, "His name's Dirk. Dirk Lloyd. He can't move, but we can't see anything wrong with him at all, and the boy can't seem to tell us either."

"No, not Dirk, it's Dark, and I'm not a boy!" said the boy desperately, but they didn't seem to take much notice of him. A wave of weakness came over him and he sighed resignedly. Dirk it is then, he thought to himself. For now. Until he got his powers back. Then they would know him by his full name and title, that was for sure!

"Okay, Dirk, we're going to check you out," she said. She started poking him, pushing here and there, lifting his eyelids and shining a bright light into his eyes. It was odd. Normally shining such a light into his eyes would burn the back of his brain like acid, much the same as holy water thrown into the face of a vampire. And yet he felt nothing now.

He heard the police officers talking with the man in green. They were mumbling things like, "Posttraumatic stress . . . Can't get anything out of him . . . Claims to be from another world . . . Some kind of dissociative personality disorder . . . Seems physically fine except for the paralysis . . ." and so on. It didn't make much sense to him but it seemed kind of patronizing. He'd disassociate their bodies from their personalities if his powers were working, no question!

"Right, Dirk, we're going to lift you up onto the stretcher. Everything's going to be okay," said the woman.

They lifted him with great care, which surprised him, because he expected to be roughly handled, if not killed outright. They loaded him into the back of the strange metal box they called an "Ambew Lance." Could the military unit these green-garbed humans served be the Legion of the Knights of Ambew? Inside it was also white, and very clean. The metallic smell and the hard steel racks reminded him of one of his torture chambers back home, despite the nasty clean whiteness of it all.

Perhaps that was it. Perhaps they intended to torture him. He couldn't see any lances anywhere, though, much less an iron maiden, spiked glove, or stretching rack. Amateurs!

The man—they called the ones dressed in green "paramedics"—leaned over him with a painful-looking needle in his hand.

Ah yes, torture it is then, thought Dirk—not exactly a lance, but just as agonizing if used in the right way. He strengthened his resolve. He was the Dark Lord, after all, and he wasn't going to break easily.

"I'm sorry, but we need to take some blood tests. It won't hurt . . . much," the paramedic said.

What kind of torture is it if it doesn't hurt? But still, he didn't really want to be tortured. And what if it wasn't torture but some kind of hideous magical device for the slaying of Dark Lords?

The paramedic brought the needle closer. Dirk saw a hollow space inside it—could it be filled with clear liquid? Some kind of toxin, probably. Perhaps even water blessed at a sacred spring. By the Nether Gods, it would burn his undead veins like acid!

"Wait!" he shouted.

The paramedic paused. "Don't worry, kid, it really doesn't hurt," he said.

"I'll give you power and wealth beyond anything you've ever dreamed of," said Dirk. "A province to govern, armies to command, magic items and spells, whatever you want! Just don't kill me!"

The man laughed out loud, as if it was all a joke, and leaned forward with the needle. Dirk managed to raise a hand to ward him off, and noticed that his Ring of Power was still on his finger, even though the hand was small, pallid, and dumpy. He still had his Ring! He tried to smear the paramedic across one wall of the vehicle, using a Blast of Ravening Flame from the ring, but nothing happened.

He looked at the ring closely. Normally, mighty runes writhed and coruscated continuously around it, but now the runes were dull and lifeless; it looked more like a simple band of drab gray lead than a Ring of Power. This was the last straw for Dirk. He had invested most of his ancient power and might, gathered over millennia of magical research, into that

Ring, and it was all gone. His Great Ring was worthless, along with his robes and all his spells. How far the mighty had fallen!

Then the paramedic stuck the needle into his arm, a minor prick of almost complete insignificance compared to the full realization of his loss. Anyway, it didn't seem like torture, and it certainly wasn't life-threatening. But then he noticed they were draining some of his blood away. Of course! It wasn't about torture or death, it was about power. They were after his blood for themselves, curse them all! Who knew what kind of mighty potions, demon summonings, and black magics could be wrought with the blood of the Dark Lord? And he was powerless to do anything about it.

He glared at the two paramedics balefully. They just smiled back at him inanely, every now and then muttering platitudes like "There, there," or "Everything will be okay," or "We really ought to tell your parents—can you remember who they are?" (Fools! If only they knew how close they had come to total subjugation in the Slave Pits of Never-Ending Toil!)

The ambulance hurtled along at quite a high speed. Dirk began to realize it was actually some kind of machine. Possibly not even powered by magic at all. A remarkable feat of engineering. He vowed to have a look into this technology when he had a chance.

Extraordinary sights greeted him as he looked out the windows. Stone buildings, paved roads, hundreds of these chariot machines rushing around everywhere like gigantic buzzing steel beetles, tall poles with what looked like magical lanterns hanging from them, and people—people all over the place. This world was awash with humans, like some kind of plague. He'd have to do something to reduce their numbers. Yes, that would be fun!

Still, he'd have to be careful. It wasn't going to be as easy to conquer this land as he'd thought. These humans had learned to harness the powers of nature in ways he'd never imagined. This city was huge, a sprawling warren of rock and iron, and so many . . . what did they call them? Stores! That was it! Stores. And also what looked like signs. All over the place, with strange red or black symbols on them, some with just numbers. What did it all mean? He began to feel very tired, and he dozed off. He dreamed of world domination.

Meanwhile, back in the car parking space the boy had fallen into, a black blob of mucus spread out slowly to form a dark patch on the ground, like a small oil slick.

The Hospital Lockup

He woke to find himself in a bed, inside a small square room. He looked down at himself. He was still in the body of a human child. It hadn't been a dream, then. It was all real.

There was a large window on one side of the room with a view over the city. It was even bigger than he'd imagined when he was in the chariot of Ambew Lance. So much glass, and steel and stone. The sight actually awed him for a moment. He was going to need a horde of Orcs to conquer it all. A *big* horde.

He realized he was feeling a little better. He was able to sit up in bed. Next to him on a tray that he could swing over his lap was a meal of what looked like bread, placed on either side of some kind of meat, and a selection of odd-looking fruit. He was hungry, so he devoured it all without thinking, though it wasn't something he'd usually eat.

When he'd finished, he tried to get up. He managed a few steps toward what looked like a water basin. And then he saw it—the mirror. He looked into it and saw the face of a brown-haired, unremarkable, somewhat tubby human child of about twelve years of age. He couldn't bear the sight—where were his majestic horns, great canine fangs, and bony skull ridges? Where was the mottled skin like thousand-year-old parchment stretched across the warped and twisted skull of one who had mastered death millennia ago? No taloned, skeletal hands. No black robes and bone-encrusted helms. None of the accoutrements of an Evil One. It was too much to bear!

"Nooooo!" he cried, and he drove his fist into the mirror. The mirror cracked, but did not shatter. And suddenly Dirk felt pain in his hand. He wasn't used to that. He looked down—there was no blood, luckily, but it was the shock of realizing how pitifully weak he was that really upset him. Human children were puny.

He looked up—the cracked mirror distorted his features in a rather pleasing way: discordant, disturbed, and twisted. That was better!

The door swung open, and several adult humans entered the room. One of them, a youngish female of the species, said, "Hello, Dirk—"

Before she got any further, he interrupted, saying,

"Dark, it's Dark Lo— Oh, what's the use?" and he fell silent.

The humans exchanged "told you so" looks, and the woman continued, "I'm Miss Cloy, from social services. And these gentlemen are Dr. Wings and Professor Randle, specialists from the Child Psychology Unit. We're here to make an assessment."

Dirk scowled. Social services? Could that be some kind of legion or military service unit for cleaning out social undesirables, like humans and Elves and other pointless do-gooders? And a unit of psycho specialists! That sounded useful. Why hadn't he thought of that? A legion of insane, psychotic, berserk Orcs for instance—what a thought! There was much to be learned here. Assuming he survived this next encounter with humankind.

"Don't worry, we're here to help," said Wings.

"Of course you are," said Dirk. "Now, listen, puny humans. First, you will tell me where I am. Then you shall bring me some clothes, and my cloak, and then take me to your leader. I will accept his sworn statement of fealty immediately and take command of this city forthwith. If you disobey me, I will destroy you all."

They stared at him, dumbfounded for a moment. Wings actually giggled, until Randle glared at him and he fell silent. Dirk took this to mean that they were finally beginning to recognize the deference and respect owed to him. Or maybe not . . .

"You're in the hospital, Dirk," said Miss Cloy, "and they'll be keeping you overnight for observation. Nobody can find anything physically wrong with you, but something must have . . . umm, happened to you."

"And that's what we'd like to find out, so we can help you," said Randle.

"I warned you," said Dirk, and he raised his hands, calling forth all of the power invested in his Great Ring, intent on engulfing them in torment with the spell of Agonizing Obedience. Normally, he'd just kill them outright, but he needed some slaves to do his bidding, and the quickest way to crush them into complete submission was by the use of extreme pain.

But nothing happened. His Ring of Power was still dull and lifeless. He ran through several spells in his mind, spells of Empowerment, spells of Transmutation, of Death, Domination, and Destruction, but nothing worked. He really had lost his powers! A wave of nausea and despair washed over him. Weakly, he climbed back onto the bed.

Dr. Wings noticed the broken mirror and said, "Look, Randle, he smashed the mirror!"

"Hmm, interesting," said Randle, stroking his chin ruminatively.

Who are these idiots? Dirk thought to himself.

IF ONLY I HAD ALL MY POWERS...

Miss Cloy sat on the end of his bed. Wings and Randle pulled up chairs. Wings popped what looked like some kind of brightly colored pill into his mouth. Dirk's brow furrowed at that. Was that some kind of magic pill that would enhance his strength or give him protection against the powers of darkness? Noting Dirk's interest, Wings pulled out a package of these odd pills and offered them to Dirk.

"Chewing gum?" he said innocently.

"Ha, you won't drug me so easily, you foolish human!" Dirk replied, waving the chewing gum away dismissively. Wings and Randle exchanged an enigmatic look. Perhaps they were beginning to realize who they were really dealing with, thought Dirk.

What followed was several hours of what Dirk called "his interrogation." It was long and drawn out because they were too weak-minded and squeamish to use torture. Well, that was their problem. They asked him seemingly useless questions: Who were his parents? What had happened to him? Where did he go to school? And so on. He told them he was from another world—and tried to prove it, but they just wouldn't believe him. Nothing he tried convinced them. They ran what they called "tests." They said his intelligence was exceptionally high. Well, of course it was. They also said he trailed behind in other areas, such as empathy, socialization, and morality. Well, of course

he did! What did they expect? Such things were useless to a Dark Lord.

Then they asked him to write down exactly what
had happened to him, just before he was found in the
Savemart parking lot—which was, in fact, another one of
their "stores," rather than the citadel of a local warlord, as
he had first thought. This is what he wrote, using one of
their remarkable pens (so much more effective than the
old quills back home). He told the tale of the last thing he
remembered before his fall to earth.

Gargon had unleashed the new war
catapults I'd designed, and that so many
Orcs had worked on and died building.
Their taut cords made the ground shake
as the skies darkened with roiling,
smoke-trailing, spark-splashing balls of
blue fire. I watched the faces of the
elite knights, the White Shields, too
closely packed to turn their horses before
the barrage rained upon them. Under the
steel visors, those grim-set mouths went
slack. They knew that death was flying to
consume them.

Ah, such a glorious day! It was all
going so well.

I see the battlefield as in a mist, a

blood-red mist. We were beating them back. Those impudent fools who had marched to the very heart of my kingdom, there in the shadow of Mount Dread, in the wan light cast by the Dark Moon of Sorrows, they saw the powers at my command and their hearts were icy with fear.

But then I caught sight of that meddler, the White Wizard, Hasdruban the Pure. Across a sea of battling troops our eyes locked. I began the Incantation of the Ninth Demise. I saw that he held something—a crystal. It shone with power. I had spoken the sixth of the nine syllables that would crack his old veins and spill his blood like dust upon the wind.

Hasdruban said one word. The crystal blazed with light. And I was falling . . .

After they'd read this, Wings said to Randle that he'd noticed something significant—the White Shields.

"The elite knights of Hasdruban the Pure. Yes, what of them?" said Dirk.

"Do you know the name of the town we're in, Dirk?" asked Miss Cloy.

Town! If this was a town, what must their cities be like? thought Dirk. Orcs weren't going to be enough to conquer this land, no matter how many he bred. He'd need to enslave or persuade some humans to serve him as well or he'd have no chance.

"It's called Whiteshields," said Randle.

"And I work for the Whiteshields District," said Miss Cloy.

The blood drained from Dirk's face. This was serious. He was a prisoner of the White Shields, his most dedicated enemies, an order of hereditary paladins sworn to one thing and one thing only—his utter destruction. For millennia they had striven against him, thwarting many of his plans and stratagems, until at last they had achieved this, their final victory. And this Miss Cloy, seemingly harmless, was in fact part of the High District of the White Shields! She'd just admitted it freely. And this social services legion must be a super elite crack unit in the service of his enemy.

But why were they telling him this? Could it be that they knew his powers were so weak that they had no fear of him at all? If so, they were right. What could he do against them? All he had at hand were the powers of a twelve-year-old human boy. Still, he must not despair. Despair was for lesser creatures, not for the Lord of Darkness. He would never give up.

What he couldn't understand was why they hadn't

just killed him outright, or put him on trial, as the White Wizard before Hasdruban had tried to do—up until he'd thrown the meddling old fool into a vat of superheated lava, that is.

Eventually, Cloy, Wings, and Randle were through with him. Dirk was exhausted. As they left, Miss Cloy said something about how they'd be finding him a home to go to, and that he'd be back to school in no time. His heart sank. A home. Surely she couldn't mean a home complete with parents and all that. What a ghastly thought! And he held onto that thought as he fell into a deep sleep.

Mrs. Fenton set off in her car to go shopping as she did nearly every day. Today the parking lot was full—except for a single space. The same space that no one had parked in for days and days, the one with the strange little black oil slick that wouldn't go away, even when it rained, the one where they'd found that boy with amnesia. She reversed into the space but the car next to hers had parked rather badly, making it really hard for her to get out. And for some reason that made her mad. Really mad. So she slammed her door open, denting the other car, before stomping off to do her shopping in an angry rage. Which was unusual, for Mrs. Fenton was one of the nicest, most placid people you were ever likely to meet.

The DREAM

Dirk dreamed of a pair of golden eyes staring at him hungrily through a white fog. The eyes glowed balefully, looking for him, seeking him, hunting him. Dirk knew he had to get away, to escape those terrible, pitiless eyes, for they were coming for him and him alone. That thought filled him with terror, a dreadful fear that gripped his dark soul in a vice of horror, a fear he wasn't used to experiencing. He was vulnerable here, trapped in the body of a little human boy. He had lost his powers. This thing, this monster with its awful eyes of yellow doom—it was coming for him, and it would destroy him forever!

He woke with a start. *It was just a dream.* He'd been woken by one of the human females they called a "nurse." She placed something they called "breakfast" in front of him—eggs, bacon, toast. He realized he was ravenously hungry and dug in with a will, images of nightmarish yellow eyes already fading. He was used to the roasted flesh of his slain enemies, but for some reason the thought of that turned his stomach. He guessed that his food requirements were now governed by the needs of a twelve-year-old human juvenile. Rather dull, he thought.

Later, Miss Cloy, the local commander of the Social Services Legion, came in to see him. By then he was up and about, feeling pretty good, all things considered. He could walk, talk, and generally do everything a young human could do without feeling nauseous. If only they weren't so pathetically feeble. Why couldn't he have the body of an ogre infant or a dragon hatchling? They could tear a human in half at this age.

Miss Cloy spoke, breaking in on his musings. "Good morning, Dirk! Good news—we've been hard at work, and we managed to get a judge to sort things out last night. You have been made a ward of the court, and we'll be placing you with a foster family by the end of the day."

"Mornings are never good, Miss Cloy. And are you saying that you have somehow managed to find some kind of magical ward against my dark powers? We shall see, puny human female!" said Dirk, and he raised his hands high above his head, readying a blast of Spectral Sorcery with which to wither her utterly.

But of course, nothing happened. Dirk sat back on the bed despondently.

"Yes, very funny, Dirk. Now try not to make any jokes for a while, and listen. We're putting you with the Purejoies, a nice young couple who have one child of their own. A boy your age, called Christopher. That's nice, isn't it? Hopefully you'll be able to make friends with him."

Perhaps they have indeed managed to put in place some kind of magical warding, Dirk thought, trying to block out the inane twitterings of Miss Cloy. A ward of the court . . . The Celestial Court of the Holy Ones perhaps? That would be a very hard ward to break indeed. But he'd have to find a way.

Miss Cloy went on, "Mrs. Purejoie is a minister at the local church, and Mr. Purejoie is a doctor. Very nice people. They've got a room all ready for you. Everything's been taken care of."

"Minister? What ministry?" said Dirk. "And what arcana is he a doctor of? Sorcery? Ritual magic? What kind of thing?"

Miss Cloy looked at him oddly, unsure if he was being serious. "Er, well, he's a doctor of medicine, actually. And a minister is a priest. You know, of the church."

Dirk stared at her as he took this in. Doctor of medicine—a healer, eh? What a waste of intellect. Such a man should be easy to manipulate. But churches—that was interesting. If they have churches that means they have gods! Perhaps he could find a powerful enough god, make an appropriate sacrifice—human of course—and maybe the god would return him to his own plane, perhaps even put him back in his original body. The news was encouraging.

"Tell me about Mrs. Purejoie's temple of which she is a priestess. What kind of god does she serve?" asked Dirk. "What sacrifices does he accept? First-born sons? The hearts of those who are blameless and free of sin?"

Miss Cloy had already decided to ignore anything Dirk said that was too out there, so she simply answered the first part of his question. "Well, you'll have to ask her. First of all, it's not a temple; it's a regular church. Mrs. Purejoie will be able to tell you all about it." She gave him that look again. "Have you really never heard of church before?"

"Of course not," Dirk replied. "I was propelled here against my will from another plane, where I was a powerful and dreaded lord of many lands, as I told you, and . . ."

Miss Cloy interrupted, "Yes, dear, yes, of course. Well, right now you're a little boy, and it's time to get out of those hospital robes and into these clothes we've got you."

She dropped some dull-colored raiments on the

bed. Jeans, sneakers, T-shirt, and a jacket—all new.
"You'll like them."

Dirk stared in disbelief at the curious clothes. Rough
blue trousers, absurd white lace-up shoes, and a cheap
piece of some kind of dyed cotton. The jacket was red
and looked like something worn by the court jesters
of Old Mylorn—well, up until his Orcish Legions had
burned the place to the ground, that is.

"I will not wear such tawdry clothes," said Dirk.
"Where is my Cloak of Endless Night? Bring it to me
now, human female!" he ordered.

Miss Cloy glared at him. "Don't talk to me like that,
young man!" she snapped. "My name is Miss Cloy. You
can call me Jane if you like, but I won't put up with
being called a 'human female'! Your wizard's robe is
hanging up in your room at the Purejoies', your foster
parents."

Dirk was taken aback. Didn't she know who he
was? He began to run through various punishments
he'd put her through to correct her behavior, but he
checked himself. This was taking some getting used to,
this powerless state he was in. How odd to find himself
in the power of others! Things would have to change
somehow. Then he had another thought: foster parents. They were obviously putting him under the control of some kind of sentinel Parent known as the
Foster. He'd been imprisoned by such Parents before,

but he'd always found a way around them, no matter what powers they had. He determined that this time would be no different. For now, it was best he play along, until he could learn more about this Parent. He'd lost his powers but he still had his intellect, his evil genius! He'd find a way out of this.

"As you wish, Miss Cloy," he said in his best imperious but polite voice.

"Thank you, Dirk," she said. "I'll be back in a few minutes, once you've changed."

She left the room. Gingerly, Dirk picked up the clothes and began to dress. The jeans seemed sturdy but weren't anything close to a good set of blackened leather armor, or the chitinous hide of the giant Battle Beetles of Borion, bred over millennia by the wise men of that city. Well, until his Winged Nightgaunts had torched the city and enslaved its population, that is. He'd kept the breeding vats though.

Dirk thrust the memory aside. What use was it to dwell on past glories? He must be strong—and that meant concentrating on the problems at hand. As Dirk dressed, he could hear Miss Cloy talking to someone outside the room. He strained to hear.

She was saying, "Whatever trauma he suffered shows no sign of fading. He's still completely delusional. Still holding on to the idea that he's from another world. Makes sense really—if he's from another world he doesn't have to face the reality of this one. Whatever happened to him must have been pretty awful, the poor boy. At least he's responding to the name Dirk, and doesn't insist it's Dark anymore, so that's a sign of progress."

Then there was a man's voice—Wings's by the sound of it: "Yes, it's a fascinating case. There've been cases of dissociative identity disorder similar to this, often brought on by some kind of physical and mental trauma, but nothing where the new personality is drawn from modern mythology quite so completely! The creation of the White Shields as his enemy is inspired. Whatever his trauma was, it's almost certainly bound up with this town in some way. We should think about treatments— psychotherapy, cognitive therapy perhaps..."

Their voices faded as they walked away. Dirk felt crushed. Nobody believed him. It was obvious they simply thought he was insane. Curse the White Wizard! Hasdruban was cunning, oh so cunning. Dirk's defeat was absolute. What a cruel punishment, to be given over to his enemies in such a state that they didn't even recognize him for what he was, and treated him as though he were insane. How utterly, utterly humiliating. He was insignificant, no longer a threat, a mere nothing, a human, a human *child* even, a mad human child! It would have been better if he'd just been slain outright.

Dirk paused for a moment. Perhaps Hasdruban

hadn't killed him because he actually couldn't kill him. Perhaps he simply wasn't powerful enough to do it. That thought gave him something to hope for. Maybe this exile was the best Hasdruban could do. Resolve and determination blossomed like a black rose in his dark heart. He declaimed to himself loudly, "By the Power of the Nine Netherworlds, I shall find a way to overcome this curse and return to my land, with power majestic and potent sorceries mightier than ever before! They shall rue the day they crossed me! For I am the Dark Lord—umm . . ."

But he couldn't remember his true name and his terrible vow trailed off into vagueness. "The Dark Lord Dirk" just didn't have the right kind of ring to it.

The House of Detention

The door opened, and Miss Cloy swept in. "Come along now, Dirk, off we go."

He bridled at her rude, commanding tone. With some difficulty he was able to swallow his pride, and followed her out of the room and down the brightly lit hospital corridor. He looked up at the back of Miss Cloy's head as she walked in front of him, and began to make the movements and gestures required for the casting of various spells, like the Charm of Sudden Baldness, the Cantrip of Uncontrollable Flatulence, and the Hex of Hideous Hives.

Miss Cloy gave him a look over her shoulder. "Stop that nonsense, Dirk, you look ridiculous! And hurry up, we haven't got all day."

This just made him even more annoyed. So he moved up to the Spell of Utter Annihilation, the Hex of the Red Ague and even the Summoning of the Ravenous Ones

Die, Miss CLOY, Die!

of Gulgor who, if the spell had worked, would have eaten every living thing in a hundred-mile radius.

Shortly, he grew bored of such games and began to take notice of the hospital around him. He marveled at the size of it, and at the utter stupidity of these humans. Why waste so much wealth and resources on curing the sick or healing wounds? Much easier to simply consign those that are unable to work into the Rendering Vats, where their bodies can be turned into something useful, like candles, sausage meat, or fertilizer. And if there's a manpower problem—well, simply create more Goblins in the Warrens or more Orcs in the Breeding Silos. Hmm, but then again, you can't just breed humans when you like, because of their ludicrously inefficient reproductive processes. Dirk decided that perhaps the humans had a point. Hospitals might be useful after all.

Miss Cloy led him to her mechanical chariot in the hospital parking lot. Her car was blue. She called it a "Beetle." Though its surface was curved and armored in a way similar to that of an iridescent beetle, the similarities ended there. Where were the horned antlers, the clawed mandibles, the jointed legs, and so on? Dirk supposed that it could be useful in war but it didn't hold a candle to the giant Battle Beetles he was used to back home. Still, it looked like an interesting machine.

As they approached, the Beetle beeped and flashed a greeting at them. Aha, thought Dirk, perhaps there

NOW tHAt'S A BEEtLe!

was an element of magic to these machines after all! Somehow it had recognized its mistress. Was it inhabited by a spirit of some kind, or was there a minor demon bound into it? Fascinating!

Miss Cloy opened a door for him, and he stepped in, acknowledging the correctness and deference she had shown with a curt nod. She got into the car on the other side.

The interior was a source of amazement to Dirk. There were buttons, levers, and lights and things. And it all looked so clean and pure, put together with a standard of craftsmanship he'd never seen before. Though on closer inspection he realized most of the paneling and some of the knobs and levers could be torn off without too much effort.

"Stop that, you little vandal!" said Miss Cloy angrily. "Now sit quietly and put your seat belt on!"

Seat belt? Dirk fiddled around with the belt by his side, but then Miss Cloy gave a *tut* of irritation, leaned over, and buckled him in. Ah, thought Dirk, it was some kind of restraint device. Ha! So she feared him so much she felt the need to restrain him! Excellent. But as he settled into his seat Dirk realized the belt wasn't really very restraining, and he could unbuckle it himself at any time. Odd. So he unbuckled it. And then buckled it. Unbuckle. Buckle.

He did this several times until Miss Cloy snapped,

"We can't go anywhere unless you're safely buckled up, you little monster. Just put the seat belt on and leave it on!"

Dirk glared at her. If only she knew what a monster he really was . . . If he ever got his old powers back then one day he'd be able to show her. Great would be the slaughter on that day!

With that thought a broad smile spread across his face. Miss Cloy seemed to recoil in horror at the sight of it. Hurriedly she looked away.

Miss Cloy did something with the key in her hand, and the Beetle burst into life with a low roar, shuddering and shaking ominously. Dirk was seized by a moment of fear and grabbed onto whatever he could get ahold of.

Miss Cloy gasped in pain, and Dirk realized he'd grabbed the soft flesh of her upper arm. Even though he hadn't meant to do it, his first thought was, "Ha, suffer and die, puny human! Fear the power of the Dirk!" but then Miss Cloy did something strange. Rather than admonish him for hurting her, or blow his head off with a spell or stab him through the heart, as he would have, she held his hand gently, and said, "There, there, Dirk, it's all right. I didn't know you'd never been in a car before. It's all right to be scared, but it's perfectly safe. I've done this a thousand times. There's nothing to fear."

Dirk stared at her in surprise. All right to be scared?

What did she mean? Was this some kind of trick? To lull him into a false sense of security by seeming to care about him? By the Nine Netherworlds, what was going on?

The car lurched forward and Dirk gave an involuntary gasp.

Miss Cloy seemed to push some kind of pedal with her foot and the car stopped. "Would you rather we walked, Dirk? It's a little far from here, but we could do that," she said kindly.

Dirk pulled himself together. He was determined to put a brave face on things, to stop being a wimpy kid and to be the Dark Lord he really was. So he said imperiously, "Not at all, Miss Cloy. Proceed immediately, and crush all those that get in our way!"

Miss Cloy acknowledged his words with a nod and then muttered something under her breath, which he only just caught, "Believe me, Dirk, I've often wanted to . . ."

The car moved off. Dirk managed to get himself under control, even when they got up to the terrifying speed of what Cloy called "thirty." Of course, he'd traveled faster than that, on the backs of dragons, and such, but never with a thousand other dragons rushing around at the same time. Everywhere there were other cars, and it seemed to Dirk like each one of them *really was* trying to crush all the other ones that got in its way. It was some kind of monumentally insane free-for-all, like Orcs at a barbecue.

After a while, the Beetle rolled on its rubbery round feet into the driveway of one of the human habitations that lined so many of their streets. It looked much like all the other human dwellings they had passed.

Miss Cloy did something and the car juddered to a halt, its lights faded and all sound ceased. This was what Dirk thought of as the Beetle's "dormant state," during which it presumably dreamed its linear insectoid dreams. Miss Cloy got out of the car, and motioned Dirk to stay where he was for now. Dirk flicked an irritated glance at her. More orders.

His thoughts were interrupted by a sickeningly cheerful bell-like sound . . . Miss Cloy had pushed a button on the side of the house. A few seconds later the door opened, and a tall, thin woman with blond hair stepped out. She wore a black top with a white collar. Her clothes reminded him of the uniform of the assassin monks of Syndalos, who operated from their mountain citadel high in the Great Skyvar Range. Until he'd used the power of a meteorite to level their entire mountain and all the assassins along with it, that is.

He watched as Miss Cloy and the woman talked. After a few moments, Miss Cloy called him over.

"This is Mrs. Purejoie; she's your guardian now," she said.

The Reverend Mrs. Purejoie

Mrs. Purejoie leaned down and said in a kindly voice, "Hello, Dirk, welcome to our house. You can call me Hilary."

Her voice made Dirk think of muffins, birdsong, and little country cottages. There was nothing Dirk liked more than to see muffins snatched out of the hands of little children and devoured by greedy Goblins, birds shot out of the sky by Orc war machines, and little cottages torn to the ground by hordes of ravening Vampires.

They took Dirk inside. Cloy and Purejoie were signing various documents and papers. These humans were so obsessed with bureaucracy that Dirk wondered how they got anything done at all. Purejoie told him to look around, but not to touch anything, especially in the kitchen.

The house seemed odd to Dirk. The pictures on the walls weren't of grand conquests or defeated foes begging for mercy or scenes of apocalyptic destruction to take pride in, but rather images of nature, or a human face, or flowers and the like. What was the point of that? You could see flowers any old time. And in any case, the point of flowers was that they could be ripped up and ruined, and human faces were all over the place, more's the pity. The seats were certainly comfortable, though. There was one large leather chair that was particularly good. He resolved to note down the design, and have one built for him on his return home, but instead of leather he'd use halfling skin.

The lanterns were interesting too. He couldn't work out how to light them though. He tried a simple Finger Flame Cantrip, but no fire appeared at the end of his finger. But that was to be expected. None of his magic had worked so far.

Eventually, he found a little button and pressed it. The lamp came on! It gave off a strange bright light from inside a curious glass ball. Artificial sunlight he supposed. Probably powered by the stuff the humans called electricity. He pressed the button again. The light went off! Marvelous! He pushed it again. It came on. And again, then again, again, again! Fascinating. And again, and so on.

"Oh, do stop that, Dirk," said Miss Cloy suddenly. He turned around, startled.

"Yes, please, Dirk, don't," said Mrs. Purejoie. "You might break it, dear, if you keep doing that. They're very delicate, you know."

Dirk really hated being told what to do, especially in such a patronizing manner. But there wasn't much he could do about it. Well, not much right now, that is. So he just smiled at them. Both of them looked surprised, afraid even, and took a step back, almost in unison. Then they looked at each other.

"See?" said Mrs. Cloy.

Mrs. Purejoie looked subdued for a moment. Then she brightened up and said, "Well, we'll see what some love and kindness can do, eh, Jane?"

Miss Cloy smiled wanly at that, extended her hand, and said in a muted tone, "Good luck, Hilary . . ."

Mrs. Purejoie shook her hand, and replied, "Thanks, Jane, I'll call you tomorrow. We'll be in touch to let you know how it goes."

Miss Cloy turned to Dirk and said, "You'll be living here from now on, probably. But over the next few weeks and months you'll also be seeing quite a bit of Dr. Wings and Professor Randle, and I'll be visiting every now and then, okay?"

Dirk grimaced. "Not those two idiots again," he said. "If I had my way I'd give 'em both a session on the Racks of Pain in my Dungeons of Doom. Clear their befuddled brains."

Miss Cloy raised her eyes and sighed. "Good-bye, Dirk, and try to be a good boy," she said somewhat unconvincingly. Then she left, leaving Dirk alone with the sickeningly nice Purejoie.

Purejoie showed him around the house. It was a technical marvel. Running water, power at the flick of a switch, warmth and comfort at will. But nothing he couldn't reproduce with a spell or a bound demon. Still, it was impressive given they weren't using magic.

Then she showed him his room. Or cell, as Dirk

preferred to call it. Purejoie seemed kindly, but he couldn't forget that she was just a Guardian, whose job it was to keep him imprisoned here so he couldn't conquer the world. Her name was also significant— Purejoie. She must be a servant or follower of Hasdruban the Pure, that much was obvious. The names were too similar. It sounded just like the sort of thing Hasdruban would set up, in fact. The Guardians of Purity, or suchlike, dedicated to keeping the Dark One imprisoned for all time, blah, blah, blah.

This feeling was reinforced by the color of the walls in his room. They were white. It was probably deliberate, as a kind of punishment. And Purejoie called the curtains "coral cream," a strange way of describing such an insipid, nothing color. After she'd shown him around his pitiful little room (how he longed for his Great Hall of Gloom and his Throne of Skulls!) she left him for a while, to "settle in" as she called it. Immediately he began to play with the light switch— on and off, on and off. But after a while he got bored with that and looked around.

He was pleased to find his Cloak of Endless Night in the wardrobe as well as a selection of other clothes, mostly typical human rubbish. Only one thing—they called it a T-shirt—was the right color for him. That was black, of course. Perhaps he'd be allowed to redecorate his cell eventually. Yes, black, with bloodred trim. And some bone art, mounted on the walls here and there. Slowly Dirk began to doze off, musing on the color black and how much he loved it.

He was running, running for his life. Around him stretched a white expanse of snow, reaching in all directions under a cloud-cold, all-white sky. Behind him something was closing in on him, something terrible, something relentless, implacable. Something that would not stop until it had eaten his dark heart. He could hear its powerful, rhythmic footfalls in the snow. Desperately he looked behind him—but in the almost total whiteout of this dirty white plain he could see only a vague shape, bulleting toward him. But in that vague outline glowed two bright yellow eyes, fixed on him with terrible purpose. The white furred thing leaped, taloned claws reaching for him, eyes blazing with feral bloodlust . . .

Dirk sat up with a start, a scream of awful fear on his lips. But he stopped himself in time and no sound came. He was a Dark Lord after all, and he had his self-respect to think of. Can't be screaming out in terror at the slightest . . .

There was a creak—his bedroom door was being closed. He snapped his head around to take a look— caught in the light outside his room was a pair of blue eyes framed by blond hair disappearing into the lighted hallway. The door shut with a quiet click, and tiptoed footfalls receded down the corridor.

It seemed some human boy had been spying on him. Probably the Purejoies' son, no doubt jealous and resentful of Dirk's coming, and checking out the competition. And who could blame him? His days of independence were numbered, for the Great Dirk had come, and all would be on bended knee before him! Involuntarily, Dirk's little hand clenched into a victorious fist as he thought this.

And maybe that's what his dream had been about, he thought to himself. Perhaps he'd sensed the boy spying on him and replaced in his mind the blue with the yellow, and the blond with the white. Hurriedly Dirk checked his room and his bed for signs of interference.

Poisoned thorns in his shoes, a crossbow bolt trap in his closet, perhaps something like the Curse of the Runes of Death. Though that was probably too sophisticated for a human boy. Still, a deadly scorpion under his bedclothes, a giant constrictor snake—that kind of thing was entirely possible. But he found nothing. For a while he lay on his bed staring at the white ceiling, so much like the dirty white sky in his dream. He mused and plotted for a while before drifting off to sleep once more, this time dreamlessly.

The GUARDIANS

"Christopher, this is Dirk, the boy who's come to stay for a while," said Mrs. Purejoie.

Christopher didn't look like he was very happy with the situation. That was only to be expected, Dirk thought, but he would soon come around. All that was required from him was total obedience to the will of Dirk. Shouldn't be too hard to arrange.

"I'll leave you two alone to get acquainted. Try and be nice, Christopher!" said Mrs. Purejoie.

With that she shut the door and left them together in Christopher's room. There was an uncomfortable silence. Dirk looked the boy over. He looked like a typical human child—in other words a brainless moron, only good for menial tasks, or possibly as a sacrifice to some dark and bloody demon lord or mighty god of evil, in return for power and wealth. In that sense, he might be useful.

He had sandy-colored hair, blue eyes, and an almost angelic innocence about him. Except that he wasn't so innocent, was he? This was definitely the boy who had crept into his room last night and spied on him. Dirk would have to do something about that. And any innocence he still had left would be crushed out of him after a few lessons in the realities of life, Dirk thought to himself.

The silence continued. It seemed Christopher was trying to ignore him. This puzzled Dirk. He wasn't used to being ignored. On the other hand, he could wait. He had the infinite patience of a Dark Lord, after all.

After a while, Christopher said, "Why'd you choose my mom and dad for parents?"

"I didn't choose them," said Dirk.

"What? What do you mean?" said Christopher.

"They have imprisoned me against my will. I don't want to be here," said Dirk.

"I don't want you here either!" said Chris waspishly.

Well, of course, who *would* want a Dark Lord in their home, thought Dirk before saying, "*Bah!* I won't be here for very long, anyway. As soon as I have regained my powers, I will be returning home to my own world, the Darklands, which lie beyond time and space."

"Yeah, well, don't hang around on my account," said Chris sharply, before the corners of his mouth began to twitch into a smile. He couldn't help himself. Beyond time and space, indeed. Hilarious!

After another short silence, Christopher said, "What was your name again?"

POSSIBLE USES OF CHRISTOPHER PUREJOIE

"You may call me Master," said Dirk.

Christopher looked as if he was about to lose his temper, but then he burst out laughing.

"They said you were sort of funny!" said Chris, still laughing.

Dirk was confused. Why was he laughing? Surely he couldn't be laughing at him? That would be tantamount to suicide! Didn't he realize that? But no, of course he didn't. Dirk was just another boy to him. Hmm, he'd have to be careful here. Obviously, Christopher was a rival, and in that sense Dirk had to either destroy him or dominate him. But without any of his powers, doing either of those was going to be a challenge.

"Who are 'they'?" said Dirk.

"You know," said Christopher. "'Them.'"

"Ah," said Dirk. "You mean the High Council of the White Shields, those do-gooding so-called Paladins of Righteousness, may they all wither and die!"

Christopher started laughing again. "Yeah, them!"

"Fear not, Christopher, I shall destroy them all in good time!" said Dirk.

"Yeah, destroy them all!" said Christopher, deepening his voice and holding his hand over his mouth to make a sound as if some kind of mechanical device was helping him breathe. Then he started laughing again, pointing to a picture on the wall. The picture showed a black-helmeted, black-visored, black-robed figure holding a sword made of some kind of glowing magical force. Underneath were the words "Star Wars."

Dirk was intrigued. The figure looked very much like one of his lieutenants, the one known as the Black Slayer, second only to Gargon in the hierarchy of his armies. He'd had to keep an eye on the Black Slayer. Gargon was blindly loyal, but the Slayer was ambitious and had delusions of grandeur. He couldn't be fully trusted. But there were subtle differences between this figure and the Black Slayer. The helmet was wrong, the colors and patterns a little different and various other details weren't quite right. Still, the coincidence was remarkable! Was this some kind of message from Hasdruban the Pure, perhaps?

"Who is that?" he asked Christopher.

"Darth Vader of course, who else?" replied Christopher.

"Darth? What kind of name is that? Actually, he looks like the Black Slayer, Lieutenant of the Iron Tower of Despair, and Commander of the Legion of Merciless Mayhem. He was one of my soldiers, you know. One of my lackeys."

Christopher's face lit up with amusement. "Ha! If only he was—how cool would that be! Imagine going to school, and having Darth Vader as your personal bodyguard. Amazing!"

Dirk said, "Oh no, I wouldn't use the Black Slayer as a bodyguard. He isn't trustworthy enough. Now Gargon, yes, but . . ."

Christopher wasn't listening. He was playing out an imaginary scenario in his mind.

He spoke excitedly, "I can see it now! Watch this. This is Grousammer—that's our principal by the way."

Christopher stood up, and hunched his neck, putting on a bizarre expression of arrogant command. "Purejoie! Your homework is late—no excuses, detention!"

Then he became Christopher again. "I think not, Mousehammer! Meet my bodyguard, Darth Vader!"

Christopher put on the deep, dark voice with the breathing difficulties and said, "Your powers are weak, old man! The ability to give out detention is insignificant next to the power of the Force!"

He fell onto his bed, laughing hysterically. Dirk was obviously missing something, but he really liked the line "your powers are weak, old man," and he resolved to use it at some stage in the future.

Christopher noticed that Dirk wasn't laughing. Of course, he couldn't know that Dirk didn't laugh very often, and when he did, it was a maniacal laugh of villainous evil.

"Haven't you seen *Star Wars*?" he asked.

"No, what is it?" said Dirk.

Christopher stared at him with an expression of amazement on his face.

"It's a movie. You know—*Star Wars*. There've been loads of them," said Christopher.

"Movie? What do you mean, 'movie'?" said Dirk.

Christopher stared at him again. Dirk raised an eyebrow.

"Oh, never mind," said Christopher, shaking his head.

Suddenly a strange sound filled the air. A little block of glass and metal on the table was flashing and giving off an annoying musical trill that grated on Dirk's ears. Christopher picked it up, flipped the lid, and began talking into the box. Dirk was amazed—a communication device of some type, perhaps? What was equally amazing was that these humans had so many of them they could afford to give one to a mere man-child!

He listened to what Christopher was saying, but it was quite hard to follow, as if it was coded in places, "Hi . . . Yeah, awright . . . *Call of Honor* or *Battlecraft*? . . . Okay . . . The foster kid? Yeah, tonight . . . He's kind of funny, actually, but still, you know . . . we'll see how it goes . . ."

He glanced over at Dirk with a half smile on his face. It was a curious smile. What was it humans used to describe such things? Ah, yes, almost a *friendly* smile. People didn't normally smile at a Dark Lord. Most unusual!

"Oh, totally whacked in the head, but kind of cool in a weird kind of way . . . Yeah . . . Sure, see you tomorrow then . . . Bye." Christopher flipped the lid shut.

"That was my friend, Nutters—we've got a shared *Battlecraft* account, but we're thinking of giving the new *Call of Honor* game a try. What do you think?"

"Nutters?" said Dirk, confused.

"Yeah, his last name's Nutley. Pete Nutley, so of course we call him Nutters. Or Nuts," said Christopher.

"Of course," agreed Dirk, though he had no idea why they would do that. It seemed vaguely Orcish somehow.

Dirk continued, "And battle craft? A battle craft account? Do they teach the art of war at your school, then?"

That could be a worry. If these humans were trained in warfare from an early age, they would be even harder to defeat and conquer.

"The art of war!" laughed Christopher. "Ha, I wish they did! No, it's a game. You know—a computer game."

"Ah, a game. I see. And what is a com-pew-tar?" said Dirk.

Christopher gave him that perplexed look again. There was a knock on the door, and Mrs. Purejoie came in.

"How are we getting along, boys?" she asked.

"Well, he's a little . . . you know . . . But might not be as bad as I thought, Mom," said Christopher and he sort of made a face as if to say, "I'll give him a chance, just this once."

Mrs. Purejoie looked surprisingly pleased, as if that

wasn't the answer she'd expected. There was a moment's silence. Dirk realized he was supposed to say something. It was time to be diplomatic.

He said, "Christopher is doing well. He has the makings of an excellent lackey. I am thinking of making him Lord High Overseer of the Armies of Darkness." Yes, that should do the trick, thought Dirk—when you don't have a stick at hand, a carrot will have to do.

Mrs. Purejoie looked a little shocked at this, but Christopher said, "Lord High Overseer! Cool!" and he started laughing again. This wasn't quite the reaction Dirk had in mind, but it would suffice for now.

Mrs. Purejoie seemed rather puzzled, but she shrugged and said, "Well, at least you're getting along, I suppose. Anyway, time for supper, boys."

They went downstairs to what they called the "dining room." A portly looking human male was sitting at the table, red-haired with a ginger beard and pale blue eyes. He stood up and introduced himself. "Hello, Dirk, I'm Dr. Purejoie. You can call me Jack."

"Or Dr. Jack, as we call him around here," said Mrs. Purejoie. They all smiled at each other in a sickening display of familial love.

Inwardly, Dirk groaned. They seemed altogether far too well-adjusted for his tastes. Oh well, it was only a matter of time before he either escaped back to his own world or subjugated this one.

"So, Dirk, how was your day?" asked Dr. Jack.

"I woke in the prison you humans call the 'hospital' to find that my powers of domination and destruction had been taken away from me, probably by some kind of warding, and that I had been given over to those psychotic fools, Wings and Randle. Then the commander of the Social Services Legion lashed me into her Chariot of Combustion and drove me here, where I was given over again, this time to my Guardians, the Pure Ones, who are tasked with my imprisonment."

There was a long moment of total silence, broken by Christopher, who started to giggle uncontrollably despite trying not to.

"This isn't a prison, dear, really it isn't," said Mrs. Purejoie gently. "It's a home. You are welcome here, and we hope you'll be happy. We *want* you to be happy. Whatever it was that happened to you before . . . It won't happen again. You're safe."

Safe? Dirk thought to himself. Who were they kidding? It was only a matter of time before the torture began, he was sure of it.

Later on, after supper, Dirk spotted a piece of wood with sixty-four black and white squares painted on it. Curious carved wooden objects sat on the wooden board. On closer inspection, Dirk recognized knights and men-at-arms; a familiar sight, similar to the armies of Hasdruban.

"What is this?" asked Dirk imperiously. (Actually, he nearly always asked things imperiously.)

"It's a chess set," said Dr. Jack. "Do you want to play a game, Dirk?"

"I do not know how to play," said Dirk.

"I'll teach you, if you like," said Dr. Jack.

"It'll be bedtime soon, though," said Mrs. Purejoie.

"Oh, it won't take long, my love," said Dr. Jack. "He's only twelve, after all. But I won't be too hard on him— just show him the ropes. He might like it."

Dirk and Dr. Jack sat down facing each other, and the doctor explained the rules. Dirk was intrigued. He could see the possibilities of the game. It was well designed, with a kind of strategic purity he could appreciate.

"Okay, then. Got it?" said Dr. Jack.

Dirk nodded.

"White or black?" said Dr. Jack.

"Oh, black of course," said Dirk.

Six minutes later Dirk said, "Checkmate. You were right, Dr. Jack. That didn't take long at all, did it?"

Dr. Jack opened his mouth, and then shut it. He was speechless.

Both Mrs. Purejoie and Christopher seemed a little stunned as well. Dirk swelled with pride. He tried his evil maniacal laugh of victory, "*Mwah, ha, ha!*" but it didn't come out right. The Purejoies laughed good-naturedly at his attempt, which was a little irritating. They were

chess pieces

supposed to quail in terror, but his powers of intimidation weren't what they used to be.

"Curses," he said. "You know the most annoying thing? '*Mwah, ha, ha!*' really loses its impact when you've got a girly Elf voice."

"Well, time for beddy-byes, boys!" said Mrs. Purejoie.

Dirk put his hands over his face and groaned. Beddy-byes—how insufferably sappy, he thought.

After a tedious time of tooth brushing (at least it didn't take as long as it used to, as he didn't have to scrape and polish his fangs and tusks) and getting into "pajamas," he and Christopher were put to bed in their rooms—or cells as Dirk thought of them.

Dirk lay in bed staring at the hideously white ceiling. Then he noticed that one of the shelves in his cell had been lined with books. He got up and looked through them. Most seemed insufferably tedious. Then he found an encyclopedia. Aha! It was filled with facts and figures about this world, which would undoubtedly be useful. He was sitting in bed with the first volume propped up on his lap eagerly soaking up information when Mrs. Purejoie came in and said, "Good night, sweetie," turned off the light, and shut the door.

He gritted his teeth with suppressed anger. How annoying! Especially as he'd lost his night vision. He got up and opened one of the sickly curtains and pulled up a chair by the window. There was just enough light from

one of the magic street lanterns for him to read by. Dirk
sat up reading late into the night, hungry for knowledge, until he was so tired that he fell asleep.

*Once again the nightmare came—yellow eyes staring
at him from the whiteness, hunting for him, seeking him
out, eager to quench its thirst with his blood.*

And then brightness flooded his little cell and he woke
with a start, blinking painfully, the shreds of his dream
washed away in the morning light. Mrs. Purejoie was
sweeping back the curtains, letting in the full light of
dawn. He hated the dawn. And the sooner he could
get around to dyeing the curtains a nice, deep black,
the better.

"Wake up, Dirk. Up you go. It's your first day at your
new school, sweetheart!"

There were so many things wrong with what she'd
said, Dirk didn't know where to start. Lack of respect,
lack of the proper honorifics, insultingly calling him
a boy—and then, to top it all off, cloying, sentimen-
tal niceness! "Sweetheart" indeed! He would show her
how sweet his heart was by ripping *her* heart out and
eating it in front of her dying eyes!

He began to prepare the Claw of Ripping Death, but
then he remembered . . . He was trapped here on this
plane, in the body of a human boy and all his powers

had been stripped away from him. He slumped back in despair. And horror of horrors, he was going to have to go to school. School! A school of the dark arts might perhaps be acceptable, but surely not a school for human children! Never!

"Nooooooo!" he cried out loud without thinking.

"Now, now," said Mrs. Purejoie. "School isn't all that bad. You're going to make lots of new friends, and learn all sorts of interesting things."

Derek Smythe was blind. That day he was walking through the Savemart parking lot with his guide dog, Buster. Suddenly, the dog started to sniff the ground frantically. Derek nearly tripped over him!

Buster growled. That was unusual—Buster was one of the most placid Labradors you were ever likely to meet.

"It's the black, slimy oil slick, that's what he's sniffing!" he heard a voice nearby saying to him.

"The what?" said Derek.

Suddenly Buster began growling and barking louder than he'd ever heard before. And off he went, pulling Derek along with him. The next thing he heard was the voice again . . .

"Whoa, boy, down, whoa . . . Ooooow! My leg, my leg, the dog bit my leg! Help! Help!"

Part Two: Settling In

The School of Indoctrination

"You'll be starting seventh grade."

"That's what you think. It will not be long before you find that this year has been redesignated as 'Year One,' or Year of our Dark Lord: One, and so forth onward into the never-ending future of my Reign of Iron and Shadows!"

Dirk had been dropped off at school a short while ago, and taken to see the principal, Mr. Grousammer, who was going to register him at the school and talk him through what was expected of him. Or so Purejoie the Guardian had said. So far it'd been a boring litany of bureaucracy, rules, and what punishments he could expect if he broke them. He was glad it was almost over.

Mr. Grousammer simply raised his eyes and sighed, stroking his straggly beard like a caricature of an evil villain.

"Yes, yes, of course—they've told me about you, but

I'm not going to put up with your nonsense for long, my boy! This is Whiteshields School and we do things differently here. Dedication, efficiency, alacrity, discipline—that's our motto, and you'll do well to follow them, young man, or it's the Detention Room for you! And don't you worry—I'm not afraid to dish out punishment when it's needed, not like those politically correct do-gooders from social services! Anyway, your first class will be English. It's just there, across the corridor, Room 2A. Here's an exercise book, mostly for homework—see, on the cover, I've filled it in for you."

Dirk glanced at it. It said, "English, Dirk Lloyd, seventh grade, Teacher: Mrs. Batelakes."

Grousammer said, "All right then, run along now. Off you go!"

Dirk stared at Mr. Grousammer, unsure how to react to him. He reminded Dirk of someone he knew, but he couldn't think who, what with his talk of motto, discipline, punishment, and the like, as if he were some kind of bearded tyrant. And what did "politically correct" mean? Also, he'd just ordered him to "run along," an unacceptable method of addressing him. But he was powerless to do anything about it.

Perhaps a different tactic was in order, so Dirk tried a smile. Mr. Grousammer actually flinched for a moment, before recovering his composure, and waved Dirk out of the room. As he left, Dirk heard him muttering something about "Hannibal" and "Lecter." Wondering

The TYRANT, GROUSAMMER

what he meant, Dirk crossed the hall. Grousammer was going to be a problem, he could tell. Typical megalomaniacal, authoritarian type with a compulsion to control and command. There was room for only one of those around here, and it wasn't going to be Grousammer!

Without thinking, Dirk swept open the door to Room 2a and strode in. A human female of middling years was talking to an unruly crowd of about thirty or so human children, who looked more like a battalion of ill-trained Goblins than pupils, all dressed in their absurd Whiteshields uniforms, just like the one he'd been forced to put on this morning. The annoying tie thing was already chafing his neck like a hangman's noose.

They all turned to look at him in surprise as he declared, "I am the Great Dirk! You may call me Master!" The children burst into laughter, much to his annoyance. How disrespectful of them! The teacher looked a little annoyed as well—perhaps she recognized him for what he was, and would punish them for laughing at him. But no, she turned her ire on him instead.

"Where are your manners? Don't you know you should knock before entering a room?" she said icily.

Dirk was taken aback. Knock? What did she mean? Knock the door down with a GateShatter spell? Seemed a bit excessive, even for him, he thought to himself.

She went on. "Now introduce yourself and sit down over there," she said, pointing to a desk at the back of the classroom.

THE GOBLINS OF ROOM 2A

Dirk scowled. He was really finding it hard to get used to the fact that he wasn't in charge. He sighed, and said, "As you command, Mrs. Battle Axe. My name is . . ."

For some reason the unruly mob of child-Goblins dissolved into laughter again.

The woman looked even angrier. "It's not pronounced BA-TEL-AKS; it's pronounced BATE LAKES! Rhymes with Great Lakes, for goodness' sake . . ." The look of annoyance on her face faded into resignation. It had dawned on Mrs. Batelakes that Battleaxe would probably be her nickname at the school forever now.

"Oh, just sit down, Dirk," she said.

Dirk ambled over to his desk. He recognized his fellow prisoner of the Pure Guardians, Christopher, sitting next to him.

Christopher nodded at him, and whispered, "Welcome to school, Dirk," and gave him that friendly smile.

Dirk eyed him suspiciously. What was it he wanted, being nice to him like that? Seated on the other side of him was a young human girl. He barely noticed her as he took in the rest of the class. A typical bunch of worthless humans, he thought. But then his attention was drawn back to the girl. The way she dressed seemed all about trying to get around the constraints of the absurd school uniform, and he liked that. Her hair was dyed jet black, and dark black stuff had been smeared carefully around her eyes. She wore curious jewelry that seemed to bear runes and other magical glyphs, and her nails were also black. There was an interesting silver device through one of her earlobes. Some kind of talisman, perhaps? Her skin was very white and pale, and she wore stumpy black boots with silver buckles. Her lips were unnaturally red, as if stained with blood. In fact, if it wasn't broad daylight, he would have taken her for a Vampire. Perhaps she was, and had found some way to withstand the burning rays of the sun.

He'd worked with Vampires before—in fact, he once had an entire regiment of Vampires, mounted on Night Mares that had served him well, until Virikonus the Vampire Hunter had destroyed them all in the Battle of the Night-Made-Day.

Perhaps she could be useful to him. He leaned over and said, "Greetings, Child of the Night, I am Dirk." She looked at him in surprise, as did the rest of the class. He realized he hadn't lowered his voice, and he'd interrupted Mrs. Batelakes, who'd been going on about something tedious. The teacher glared at him, and he fell silent, feeling somewhat confused with the whole situation.

A bit later, the Vampire girl leaned over and whispered, "Hi, I'm Susan—you can call me Sooz. Child of the Night—I like that!" She smiled at him. Dirk nodded graciously, as if taking a compliment from one of his servitors.

After the class was over—an interminable time of

droning tedium for Dirk—he and Christopher were standing together outside the classroom. Christopher was explaining things to Dirk.

"Yes, every day during the school year, we have to sit in rooms like that, and the teachers tell us things we have to learn—that was English. There's also math, social studies, language arts, science, and PE. Then, when we get home, we have to do more stuff, called homework."

Dirk's jaw dropped. He stood aghast at the thought of the endless hours of tedium ahead of him. This was like some kind of never-ending, hideous torture! Days of droning drudgery appeared before him in his mind's eye, stretching away forever. Not even he, a past master at inventing cruel and unusual punishments could have come up with something like this!

Then the human girl called Sooz came up to them and said, "Hi, Chris. Is this the one staying at your place?" She looked Dirk up and down appraisingly.

"Yup," said Chris.

"And is he . . . Well, you know, the psychologists and everything?" she said.

"Oh yes, completely!" said Chris emphatically.

"Cool!" said Sooz.

"Tell me, Child of the Night, how can one such as you withstand the bright, burning rays of the pain-giving Sun? Has there been some breakthrough in Vampiric Lore among the Clans of the Undead?" Dirk asked.

SOOZ, the CHILD OF THE NIGHT

Sooz stared at him for a moment, as if not quite sure whether or not he was mocking her. But then she laughed out loud. "You're being serious, aren't you? Ha—I love it!" she said.

"Told you!" said Christopher.

"Of course I'm serious. Why wouldn't I be? Surely you are a Vampire, are you not?" said Dirk.

Sooz laughed some more, grinning from ear to ear. "No, I'm not a real Vampire, fudge boy—I'm a Goth!"

"A Goth? What is this Goth thing?" said a bemused Dirk. "And what is a fudge boy?" Sooz stopped laughing, and looked at him as if he was crazy, a look Dirk was getting very used to.

"You really don't know, do you?" she said.

"No, I do not. I am new to this plane and there is much I need to learn. However, I should warn you that it is only a matter of time before I subjugate your world under the heels of my all-conquering boots!"

Christopher and Sooz glanced at his white sneakers and burst into laughter.

"You're hilarious," said Sooz, wiping tears from her eyes. "I like you!"

Dirk was flabbergasted. She "liked" him! How extraordinary! People didn't "like" him. They were supposed to fear and hate him, to feel terror at his coming, to bow down before his might like the gazelle before the lion, not *like* him.

"So, what is this Goth thing then? Explain, Night-walker!"

Again, this made Sooz grin all over.

She said, "Well, Goths are people who follow a particular fashion style. But it has to be Gothic—you know, some Victorian looking stuff, horror movies, maybe a Vampire look, which I'm so pleased you noticed. And a particular kind of music—heavy metal sometimes, or grunge, or some indie bands, and death rock. But mostly for me, straight up Goth bands like AngelBile and The Demonfires. Goths are kind of, well, *different*, like outsiders. We don't fit in with normal people. Or 'Normies' as I call them."

Dirk latched onto something she'd said, "Death Rock? A Rock of Death? Where is this Rock, and how can I bind its powers to my will?"

Chris and Sooz were laughing again.

"No, no," said Sooz. "Rock *music*, fudge boy!" she said, playfully giving him a light slap on the arm. "Death rock is a return to the old classics that started the whole Goth music scene, like Siouxsie and the Banshees and The Sisters of Mercy. Who are way cool by the way, even if they are kind of old."

Dirk looked away, completely stunned for a moment. She had actually laid hands on him. Nobody laid hands on him! Ever! And she'd called him a fudge boy. Twice! Presumably it was some kind of compliment or statement of worship. Possibly. Or maybe not—he wasn't sure. He felt anger rise in him, and he raised his hands to cast the Raiment of the Cockroach spell—a brief period as an insignificant insect would teach her proper respect. But he thought better of it, and managed to overcome his anger, forcing it down. He lowered his arms. He had no power anyway, and he couldn't afford to alienate these two, his only real interface with this strange new world—even if they were only children.

The adults simply thought he was crazy or treated him like a difficult child—these two, although they might laugh at him, at least treated him like an equal. He was coming to realize that he was going to have to learn new ways of dealing with things, and this Sooz could be useful to him. So for the time being he would have to live without the level of respect he was used to.

Best to continue as if nothing untoward was going on. Dirk said, "I see. You mean they are musicians? And angel bile? That would make for a powerful spell component I'm sure, if correctly harnessed to the dark side. As for a demon fire, I already have one of those burning, in the catacombs beneath my Iron Tower of Despair."

"No, they're just bands too!" laughed Sooz.

"Bands? Like a band of Orcs, or something?" said Dirk, still confused.

This caused further laughter. "No, no," said Christopher, "they're musicians, a music band."

"Ah, I see. Musicians. *Hmph*. What a shame. Still,

this Goth 'fashion' sounds interesting. I too am an outsider. Also, I like the look. Much more in keeping with my own tastes. Perhaps I shall become a Goth too. What do you think, Christopher and Sooz?"

"That'd be great," said Sooz smiling.

She looked genuinely pleased, which was strange. Most people, even Orcs—no, even powerful Vampire Lords—would be a little uneasy about him, a Dark Lord, joining their group. But I suppose to this human girl I am just another human boy, Dirk thought.

"You'd better check out the music first, in case you don't like it," said Christopher. "I've got a Morti clip on my phone you can listen to, though it's not really Goth music, but sort of related."

"Oh no, not Morti," said Sooz, raising her eyes to heaven. "Much too heavy metal for me! It's not Goth music, but yeah, see what you think."

Christopher took out his cell phone, and a loud thrashing noise, like the sound of rusty armor being scraped clean by a hundred Goblin slaves, intermixed with the bursting rhythms of the dragon's heartbeat came out of the little device.

"Hmm, catchy," said Dirk. "It reminds me of home."

Chris smiled and said, "Here, there's a little video clip, look."

Pictures formed on the small surface of the phone. Aha, thought Dirk to himself, it was more than just a voice teleporter, but also a Scrying Crystal. Except

it wasn't a crystal of course, but one of these technical machine things these humans seemed so good at,
according to the encyclopedia he'd been reading. He
had to strain his eyes a little, but he could just about
make out the pictures.

But then Dirk gaped in astonishment. Standing in
front of a few undead, or perhaps demons, was Gargon,
his most loyal retainer! And he was *singing*—he didn't
know Gargon could sing!

"By the Nine Netherworlds, it is Gargon himself!"
yelled Dirk, "My lieutenant, Dread Gargon, the Hewer
of Limbs, Captain of the Legions of Dread! This scrying
device must somehow be accessing my own world. What
kind of magic is this? Look, look, it's Gargon!"

"No, no, that's Morti, the lead singer," said Chris. "It's
from a concert in Finland. They're Finnish, you know."

Dirk spoke heatedly. "Fin Land? Finnish? Some
kind of land beneath the sea, peopled by fish beings?
What are you saying?! Gargon isn't some wretched
Merman or an Undine or something; he's the offspring
of the foul and unholy union of a Demon Lord and a
Lich Queen, and he's my most loyal servant! He hates
the sea! Ah, Gargon, I need you!"

Sooz and Christopher started laughing again. Dirk
glared at them. It didn't have the desired effect—i.e.
all-consuming terror—like in the old days, but at least
they tried to stifle their laughter.

"Sorry, Dirk, sorry. You're just so funny some-times—that's why we like you! Anyway, Finland is in Europe—and it's full of people just like here; it's not under the sea at all. Just a regular place. Well, sort of," said Christopher, grinning again.

"And he's just a man dressed up to look like that, Dirk—though I like the Lich/Demon thing! Sounds cool."

"No, it is him. It must be. He's the spitting image of him," replied Dirk. "He must have found a way to get to this world on his own—which is surprising. He's not known for his initiative, just blind obedience. Still, he has done well. He must have put a rescue mission together—it's obvious he's managed to get here with-out suffering the catastrophic body change that I have. We must find him. Take me to him immediately."

Sooz shook her head, "Can't be done, I'm afraid. He's miles and miles away, and we've got no way of getting there. We're only kids."

"Actually," said Chris, "there's a Morti concert in town in a couple of months. We could get tickets and go see them."

"Excellent! That is good, Christopher, very good. If you can arrange this, you will be rewarded."

Christopher looked a little miffed at that. "I don't want a reward, Dirk. This is just normal stuff that friends do for each other," he said.

"Friends. Hmm, that is not a word I am very familiar with. But I have a vacancy for a lickspittle if that's what you mean," said Dirk, in his most imperious voice.

Dirk seemed surprised when they both burst out laughing again. Then Sooz noticed his Ring.

"Wow, that's cool! Where did you get it? It's really Goth," she said.

Dirk said, "This? It's not cool, or even cold. It's my Great Ring, my Ring of Power. I forged it millennia ago, in the fires of the World's Heart, deep beneath the ground. But now it has lost all its power. It is worthless! Here, take it." He pulled it off his finger and gave it to Sooz. She grinned and actually jumped up and down with excitement. Odd little creature, thought Dirk to himself. But amusing.

Sooz held it up to the light. "What's that on the front? Some kind of signet symbol, like a skull or a face. And those carvings on the inside—like runes or something. They look great," she said as she slipped the ring onto her finger. "It fits perfectly and goes so well with my bracelets." She held her hand out to admire it.

"The stylized face is my coat of arms, my seal. The runes are ancient though—the language of magic itself, from before the world was made," said Dirk. "Well, my world that is, I've no idea about this strange place."

"Cool!" said Christopher.

"Yeah, nice!" added Sooz. The runes looked a bit like this:

ᛏᚻᛗ ᚷᚱᛗᚨᛏ ᚱᛁᛏᚷ ᚯᚠ ᚲᚯᚹᛗᚱ

The seal on the front of the ring looked like this:

Sooz loved it. "Thank you so much, Dirk, thank you!" she said, and she leaned forward and gave him a little kiss on the cheek.

Dirk recoiled for a moment. As far as he could remember, he'd never been kissed before. Granted, he couldn't remember all the way back to his beginning, but he certainly hadn't been kissed for several thousand years or so. His face was getting hot.

"Your face is all red," said Christopher.

"He's blushing," said Sooz, giggling.

"Blushing? What is this blushing? Have you laid some kind of curse upon me with the kiss of the Vampire?" said Dirk accusingly, but this only made Sooz giggle even more.

"I'll tell you all about it later," said Christopher.

Sooz reached into her backpack. Dirk noticed there were words written on it. It said, "Angelbile, Demons of Destruction tour" in red lettering that dripped blood.

"Nice bag!" said Dirk, without thinking.

"Thank you, Dirk," said Sooz. She handed him a book. "Every gift deserves a gift in return. This is a diary I just bought, but I haven't started it yet. It's a Goth diary, of course, but I'm sure you'll like it. You can write down all your thoughts and dreams in it."

The book was black. That was good. On the front was an embossed figure of what looked like Death himself. Underneath it said, "The Grim Reaper Diary." It reminded Dirk of some of the books he used to have in the Dark Library in his Iron Tower, like *The Book of Bringing Forth the Dead*, or his first-edition copy of *The Ultimate Necronomicon*.

"Thank you, Sooz. It's beautiful," said Dirk, genuinely pleased. This was the best thing anyone had ever given him so far on his travels in this strange land. "It's . . . er, well, it's cold. Er, I mean cool," he said. This drew more laughter from Chris and Sooz.

Then the bell rang for the next class. On the way in to the classroom, Dirk whispered in Christopher's ear, "What is this 'cool' thing, and what is this 'fudge' term she uses? Presumably it is some kind of honorific?"

Christopher laughed. "Cool is slang for 'great' or 'good,' and fudge is . . . Well, it's named after low grades— you know, F for fail, U for unsatisfactory, or a D grade and so on. Basically, she was calling you stupid!"

Dirk sighed. There was so much to learn in this strange place.

Later, when he was taken back to the Pure Guardian jailers after school, he sat on his bed, and wrote in his diary for the first time. He decided to call it:

My BLACK DIARY of Doom

And this was his first entry:

February 1

I have lost my powers. My armies
of Goblin-kind, my Legions of Dread,
my squadrons of winged demons, are
gone. The Ring of Power is dead,
and I have given it up. My Cloak of
Endless Night is worthless. The
Helm of the Hosts of Hades is lost
or destroyed along with my Ebon
Staff of Storms. The White Wizard's
spell has regressed me into the body
of a child. But the senile old fool has
made a glaring oversight—he has
left my mind unaffected. I still
possess my dark intellect, my genius
for stratagems, my arts of alchemy,
artifice, and persuasion. And my capacity
for infinite patience . . .

A few days later, he wrote another entry:

February 7
The nightmares are getting worse. I
have at least one a week. The White
Hunter is closing in. I know it wants
to hunt me down, to rip out my heart
and eat it. What can I do to protect
myself?

And then another one. He was beginning to rather
enjoy keeping a diary, especially when he could vent
some anger . . .

February 8
Today I received a report card from
those insufferably arrogant and
interminably irritating humans they
call "teachers"! As if they could teach
me anything! I, the Dark Lord, Master
of the Legions of Dread and sorcerer
supreme! It is I who should be teaching
them! Teaching them the value of
subservience, of obedience to the will
of a superior being, for a start.
Teaching them to grovel before me
like the lickspittle dogs they are!
     I have attached the report here in my
diary, as a perpetual reminder of the need
for revenge!

Whiteshields School Report: DIRK LLOYD, 7th Gr.
Teacher: Mr. Grout

Social Studies	Needs regular help to ensure progress at times	Making progress with some help overall	Making satisfactory progress overall	Making good progress	Achieves a consistently high standard overall
KNOWLEDGE OF PERIOD STUDIED					✓
HISTORICAL INQUIRY & SKILLS					✓
RECORDING & PRESENTATION OF WORK			✓		

EFFORT	Needs to improve	Varies	Satisfactory	Good	Very good	Excellent
		✓				

Teacher's comment:

Dirk is a difficult pupil. Certain areas of history simply do not interest him, like social history or the industrial revolution. However, wars, massacres, atrocities, and political infighting fascinate him. He is the best pupil I have when it comes to military history. His presentation is poor, because he often hands in his homework in novel ways. A replica Roman helmet with a bloodstained gash, and candy "brains" dribbling out, is all very well, but I had asked for a written report on Caesar's Gallic wars.

February 13
I have come up with a suitable plan of
vengeance for this report card business.
I shall steal a blank report card and fill it
in from my point of view—no wait, from

the point of view of all the inmates of the
school, the pupils, as if we were making
a report on the absurd antics of our
teachers, instead of the other way
around! Hmm, especially that tyrannical
fool, Grousammer. Yes, a report on the
principal! I will then make many copies,
and put them up all over the school! They
shall rue the day they dared to judge me,
just you wait and see! Mwah, ha, ha!

February 14

Even more galling than the report card
debacle, that accursed madman, Mr. Banks—
the human children call him "Sandy"—the
geography teacher, gave us a special
project, to draw up a map of the town we
live in—or in my case, have been exiled to.
Anyway, I completed the task to a level of
excellence beyond the abilities of any of my
"classmates" but that dimwit Sandy still gave
me a detention for it! Why can these fools
not recognize genius when they see it?
Here is the map, as proof of my genius and
the cruel injustice of my punishment. Well,
not really cruel, more of an inconvenience.
These milksop humans don't have any idea
how to truly punish someone!

A MAP OF THE TOWN OF WHITE SHIELDS

The Court

Getting used to life on earth was hard for Dirk. He had to go to school, minimize the number of detentions he was given, avoid the likes of Grousammer the principal, the White Shields High Council, the Social Services Legion and those psycho fools, Wings and Randle. He marked off the days of grueling drudgery in his own way:

February ~~18~~

I hate the way they date things here.
When I take over, I'll change the months'
names. February—when I came to this
land of do-goodery—I'll change to Fall—
heh, that'll confuse the humans. March,
April, and May will be Doom, Gloom, and
Dismay. Much better names for those
human-loved months of spring, eh?

February FALL 28

I have gathered together the first of my followers. Every day at that Dominion of Doom the humans call "school," Sooz and Christopher meet with me during breaks. We have formed a kind of clique that I call the "Dark Lord's Court in Exile." The Child of the Night, Sooz, and the Son of the Pure Guardians, Christopher, are my lieutenants, my lickspittle courtiers. However, Sooz and Christopher do not seem to see it that way. Christopher said the other day it was because it was, "Fun, and we like hanging out with you, dude, pretending you're a Dark Lord."

Fun? Hanging out? Pretending? And what is this "dude" term I hear so much of? In any case, it is becoming obvious that they do not understand their true positions in my court. They seem to spend most of their time laughing when we are together.

Nevertheless, there must be some recognition of my power and status, for other human children are trying to get into the Dark Lord's Court in Exile.

March Doom 7

My court is growing. My chief courtiers,
Chris and Sooz, are the inner circle
but others come and go all the time,
like Chris's friend "Nutters." All of them
seek to bask in the royal glow of the
Great Dirk. Some even call me the Lord
of Darkness, or other titles I subtly
suggest, like Sorcerer Supreme, the
Dark One, and Master of the Nine
Netherworlds. But most prefer to
name me after something the Child of
the Night came up with, the title "The
Lloyd of Dirkness." At first I wasn't
sure whether to be angered. But I have
to admit, it did make me laugh, and it is
obvious that those who address me as
the Lloyd of Dirkness seem to do so
with respect. And affection, which is
somewhat annoying. I earn my respect
through fear! I rule through terror!
By the Nether Gods, people aren't
supposed to like me!

Still, for now it is the best I can do,
and I am beginning to enjoy our courtly
meetings. I haven't laughed so much in
two thousand years.

March Doom 17

There are problems. My fame has attracted the attention of larger, more aggressive children. Sooz calls them mindless bullies. I call them Ogres. I have seen their type before, all over the Darklands. Normally they are easy to control, but unfortunately I do not have my ancient powers and I cannot coerce them to my will as I once did.

There are those who mock—we can handle them with some astute, waspish replies of our own. But these bullies can get what Christopher calls "really nasty," with pushing and shoving, the ripping of bags, snatching of books or phones, and even the occasional raised fist and shove, with worse threats to come. Of course, it is nothing compared to battling the Archangels of the Celestial Court of the Holy Ones, or struggling with the White Wizard for millennia. But still, to my followers this "mindless bullying" seems important, for they know naught else.

And I'm still getting those terrible nightmares, or "whitemares" as I like to call them. It feels like the White Hunter is closing in. And to top it all off, another

report card! Blast those do-gooding
teachers, may they rot forever in my
Dungeons of Doom!

Whiteshields School Report: *DIRK LLOYD, 7th Gr.*
Teacher: *Miss Barnes*

SCIENCE	Needs regular help to ensure progress at times	Making progress with some help overall	Making satisfactory progress overall	Making good progress	Achieves a consistently high standard overall
KNOWLEDGE AND ITS APPLICATION					✓
UNDERSTANDING & CARRYING OUT INVESTIGATIONS					✓
INTERPRETING RESULTS & DRAWING CONCLUSIONS					✓
RECORDING & PRESENTATION OF WORK			✓		

EFFORT	Needs to improve	Varies	Satisfactory	Good	Very good	Excellent ✓

Teacher's comment:

Dirk is a difficult pupil. But he is also one of the most gifted science students I have ever taught. The real problem isn't to do with his learning or aptitude for science; it's what he wants to do with his talents. "Creating the most deadly toxin known to man" is hardly a suitable subject for a science project. And making his own brand of superglue and using it to stick the principal's shoes to the assembly room rostrum nearly got him expelled.

March Doom 17

Things are getting worse. The mindless Orc bullies are beginning to pick on me! The outrage! They are making comments like "There goes the Dork Lord!," or "There goes 404!" or "Hey, it's Looney Toons," or "Yo, Dirk, what's it like to be a nutjob?"

I am beginning to master that wonder of wonders—computer technology—so I know what 404 is, but what are Looney Tunes? I will ask Christopher—he will know.

Anyway, the point is that I am not being addressed in the correct manner—I'm not getting the respect I deserve. In fact, they are "dissing" me, as Sooz calls it. Nearly every day. This is intolerable and cannot go on. I will have to do something about it. And I think I know what.

The next day at school, Dirk was walking down the corridor to class. Up ahead loomed the worst bully in the seventh grade, Phil Miller, and his two friends, Dave Murray and Jon Chu. Phil Miller was a big guy, much bigger than Dirk by a long shot. They stopped in the middle of the corridor, blocking it off. Dirk raised his eyes, shook his head in contempt, and tried to get past them, but Phil Miller shoved him back, saying, "Oh no, not so fast, Dork Lord, ya wacko nerd!"

PHIL MILLER

"Get out of my way, brainless one," said Dirk. Even though Phil Miller loomed over him like an Ogre over the tiniest Goblin, Dirk was not intimidated in the slightest. This seemed to enrage Phil Miller even more—why wasn't this little squirt afraid of him?

"You little freak!" he shouted and gave Dirk another aggressive shove in the chest.

Dirk narrowed his eyes angrily, and said, as loudly and as clearly as possible so that everyone in the nearby vicinity could hear him, "I think it was particularly nice of you to stay at home yesterday to help your mom ice that cake, Phil, instead of playing soccer with your friends."

Phil Miller's jaw dropped. "How did you know . . . ," he spluttered.

"That sugary pink heart was a nice touch—your little sister's girlfriends will love that," added Dirk.

Jon Chu sniggered. Dave Murray, however, looked a bit annoyed. "You said you couldn't make soccer 'cause you were grounded for smashing a window," he said, pointing an accusing finger at Phil.

"No, I . . . I *was* grounded!" protested Phil, caught off guard.

"Pink sugar icing," said Jon, laughing. "That's really girlie!"

"No, no . . . Anyway, it wasn't pink, it was red!" said Phil.

"So you *did* stay in and ice a cake instead of playing soccer!" said Dave.

"Er . . . umm . . ." Phil Miller went bright red.

"Mama's boy, huh?" quipped Jon.

The exchange continued, with Jon and Dave increasingly ragging on Phil. While this was going on, Dirk quietly went on his way. When he'd reached the end of the corridor, Phil shouted after him, "I'm going to get you for this, dork boy!"

"Perhaps your friends would like to hear about those Power Rangers pajamas you still keep under your pillow?" replied Dirk instantly, making sure there wasn't a shred of fear in his voice. This caused even more laughter, and also had the added effect of shutting Phil Miller up.

This altercation with Miller soon went around the whole school—how Dirk had shown him up just with words. There were a few more attempts by Phil Miller types to pick on Dirk, but these soon stopped because every time they came at him or called him out, he'd reveal something really, really embarrassing about them. It just wasn't worth it. Nobody could figure out how Dirk knew all this stuff about people—but he did, and it was always true.

One day, Christopher and Sooz had asked Dirk how he'd found out all those personal things about people.

"Necromancy," said Dirk matter-of-factly. "The dead know all that passes on this plane—it's just a question of summoning forth the spirits of the slain and forcing them to tell you their secrets."

"Right, of course—how could it have been anything

else!" Christopher had replied, and they'd all laughed. And that became the official story around the school. Even though nobody really believed it, of course.

Dirk was beginning to make a place for himself in his own way. However, there was one group he was still having trouble with—the jocks, as they called themselves.

You had to be really good at sports to get in with the jocks. They looked down on anyone who wasn't, and they particularly liked to pick on the nerds. And Dirk was a bit of a nerd. He was learning all about computers really fast, and he was already champion of the school chess club. He loved super-nerd stuff like the card game Magic and interactive game books and fantasy role-playing games. "Why is the Dark Lord always the bad guy?" he was often heard to say, in genuine puzzlement.

And Dirk wasn't any good at soccer or baseball, or any other sport. He claimed it was because he couldn't get used to being in the body of a weak human child, and that he missed his horns, his great fangs, and his superstrength. Everyone else claimed it was just because he was terrible at sports.

The leader of the jocks was Sal Malik and he was captain of the Whiteshields baseball team. He was also very good-looking and a black belt in karate. Most of the school looked up to him. One day, Dirk was up for selection for the baseball team, though it wasn't an official game, just tryouts and practice. Dirk hated waiting with the other kids to be chosen—he was usually one of the last to be picked and he found it unnecessarily humiliating. After all, he should be the one doing the humiliating, not the other way around. He didn't even like playing these stupid games, anyway.

Of course, it'd be different if he had a team of Ogre football players, a supervillain soccer team or Vampire baseball squad for instance. The idea threw up some interesting questions. Is drinking the blood of the opposition classed as foul play? A pack of Ogre forwards would make for an unstoppable line, but would they allow it? Would Dr. Octopus make the best goalie?

He'd considered just not turning up, but cutting class would only lead to more attention from the likes of Miss Cloy, and those Child Psycho fools, Wings and Randle, and he could really do without that. So he just put up with it. Eventually, he was the last boy standing and Sal Malik was forced to choose him for his team. Dirk felt angry and humiliated, but kept it to himself. Instead he began to put together elaborate revenge fantasies in his head, which made him feel a bit better. It was something he'd been doing a lot of recently.

The game began—Sal's team was fielding, and Dirk was sent off to a corner of the outfield where it was thought he could do the least damage. Dirk did what he usually did in these circumstances—he began to have daydreams (or daymares as he preferred to call them), thinking up complex schemes of world domination, coups, and hostile takeover bids and the like. But then the batter actually hit the ball toward him. Dirk had to pick up the ball and throw it back—all too slowly, unfortunately, judging by some of the comments from his teammates, but at least this time he didn't fumble it. This caused him to take an interest in the game, and he began to notice a few things.

During a break for drinks, he went up to Sal and said portentously, "Sports Lord Sal Malik, listen to my words!" Sal stared at him blankly. Dirk had his attention, so he fell back into a more normal idiom—something he'd been working on recently—saying, "That batter we can't seem to get out—he's left-handed, isn't he?"

Sal looked at him, one eyebrow raised inquisitively, as if he still didn't quite believe that Dirk had actually spoken to him.

Dirk went on. "Well, he seems to be really good with that wooden club . . . Umm, I mean bat, on the, umm, what do you call it—inside corner. That's where most pitchers throw the ball normally, against right-handers, so he's practiced with that. Why not give Brownie a try at pitching—he's slow, but accurate, and tell him to aim for what would normally be the inside if the batter is right-handed. It ought to tempt him into taking some big hits, and his stance is really off on that side. Might get a strike or two, and the chance for an out."

Sal frowned. Not only could he not believe that Dirk

had actually spoken to him, he couldn't believe what he'd actually said either—after all, nerds aren't supposed to know anything about sports, right?

Dirk went on. "Move a couple of field slaves out that way," he said, pointing to places in the outfield.

Sal's eyes followed his finger. "Oh, you mean shift the centerfielder," said Sal, automatically processing the tactical thinking suggested, despite his surprise.

"Indeed, as you say," said Dirk.

Sal stared at him in astonishment some more, and then his eyes narrowed in thought and he went off to talk to some of his team. When the game restarted, Dirk was gratified to see Sal making the changes he'd suggested. And lo and behold, the batter flied out, almost exactly as Dirk had predicted!

As the game progressed, Sal actually asked for Dirk's advice on several occasions, and most of the time what Dirk suggested made sense. After all, he did have an innate grasp of strategy, and it served him well. They won the game in the end, and Sal wasn't so proud or arrogant that he couldn't see that Dirk had had a lot to do with it. Winning was everything with Sal, and he wasn't going to miss out on a chance to improve his performance as captain just because the advice he was getting was from a nerdy geek.

So Dirk and Sal struck up an unlikely friendship. They'd meet, as if by accident, though both had kind of tacitly arranged it. Sal didn't want the jocks to know he was buddies with the "uber-Nerd King." So they'd sort of "bump into each other" at the vending machine, or by the back wall of the school that overlooked the garden, as if they both happened to be there at the same time "admiring" the principal's vegetable patch (i.e. dreaming of ways they could get in there and rip it up; Grousammer's patch had been trashed so often he'd actually put barbed wire around it in an attempt to keep the vandals at bay).

Sal and Dirk would discuss sports—but not in an "I support the Dodgers, and hate the Angels" or "There's only one Albert Pujols" kind of way, but really serious talks about tactics and strategy, especially baseball and soccer—Sal's main interests. Dirk studied these sports carefully—it was important to him that he cultivate this relationship with Sal. It was a way of getting full acceptance in school, and once he'd achieved that he'd have the perfect platform on which to build his power base.

So Dirk got better and better at tactics. After a while, he found that team captains were selecting him first because his strategic knowledge was so valuable. Sal even made Dirk his cocaptain. Sal was like King Arthur, and Dirk was his Merlin. He even tried to get Dirk onto the squad, but that wasn't possible, as the coach did the selection, and no matter how you played it, Dirk simply wasn't good enough to be on the team as a player in his own right. So far, anyway. But he was good enough to be the official scorer, so he was always on the sidelines,

SPORTS LORD SAL MALIK

ready to give Sal advice on where to position himself, or how to exploit weaknesses in the opposition's lineup.

Dirk was quite satisfied with his position as cocaptain/adviser/Merlin. Of course, he would have preferred to be in total command, but he recognized he didn't have the physical skills necessary for such a role. But he had considerable influence, and pulling the strings in the background suited him well. More important, he and Sal became friends of a kind, and it gave him protection, and even influence, with the jock types. It was a very important strategic alliance for Dirk.

The school won more and more games and was closing in on first place.

Sal became more and more reliant on Dirk so their relationship began to change subtly. Dirk began to get the upper hand. No longer were meetings "held in secret."

Instead, Sal had to come to Dirk to be part of his Court, hanging out with the likes of Sooz, Christopher, and various others like Chess wizards, Warhammer nerds, computer freaks, role-playing gamers, Goths, and so on.

So it was Dirk that forged a position for himself in school. Dirk commented on it in his own way in his diary:

March DOOM 2?
Christopher can be very useful at school.
He explains my commands well to my

assembled lackeys. They don't all do as they are told—in the good old days I would have simply destroyed one of them as an example to the others. The human girl called Sooz does well though. Christopher tells me she has a "crush" on me. I thought he meant she was going to try and crush me in some kind of coup but he has explained that this means she "likes" me. As far as I can tell, this will be very useful. She will obey my commands, not out of fear, but because she actually wants to. Perhaps I can use this as a new way of getting what I want.

Anyway, I have rewarded Christopher by naming him as my chief lieutenant, but he still refuses to call me "Master." Normally I would punish him, but unfortunately I need him to help me make sense of this strange world. Perhaps if I conquer earth, or take him with me back to the Darklands, then I can punish him fittingly. But for now I must be "nice" to him. Which is difficult for me.

In the meantime I have come up with an excellent plan for the conquest of the school.

PLAN FOR WHITESHIELDS SCHOOL MILITARY COUP

Notes:
1: Must find a way to bring an army of
Orcs, Goblins, and Nightgaunts to earth.
Breed them here, perhaps?

Sooz's phone thrashed out the latest AngelBile track she had as her ringtone, a song called "I Can't Die, If Dying Is Without You," currently number two on the Gothic music charts. She looked at the caller ID and picked up.

"Hi, Chris," she said brightly.

"Hi, Sooz," said Chris. "Guess what?"

"What?"

"My dad got me some Morti tickets! Do you want to go?" said Chris.

"Morti! Gah! I dunno . . . umm . . . is Dirk going?" said Sooz.

"Well . . . yeah, he is," said Chris.

"Oh, okay then, I'd love to come," said Sooz.

"So, you wouldn't have come if Dirk wasn't going, is that it?"

"No, no, of course I would have!" said Sooz unconvincingly.

"Yeah, right," said Chris bitterly.

"No, really, honest! Umm . . . anyway, did you hear about the report card on the principal?" said Sooz, changing the subject.

"Yeah, I heard," said Chris, still a bit miffed, but

getting caught up in the excitement of the whole episode—the story was going around the school like wildfire, along with many photocopies of a report on the principal, a pretty rude report. "Fantastic, wasn't it? Mousehammer completely lost it when he saw it, didn't he?"

"It was Dirk, wasn't it? That's what they're saying at school," said Sooz.

"Yeah, it was him all right," said Chris. "He stole a report card and filled it in himself."

"He stole one? How?" said Sooz.

"You won't believe it! You see, he told me he'd managed to get some kind of spell or something to work. Or to put it in Dirk-speak, it went something like this, 'My evil genius knows no bounds for I have managed to get one of my spells—the spell of the Sinister Hand—to work here on this benighted plane you puny humans call earth. *Mwah, ha, ha!*'"

"Ha, ha, that's good Chris, sounds just like him! So what does it do, this spell?" said Sooz.

"It's really weird. He says it lets him detach his left hand and send it off on its own."

"What? Gross!"

"Yeah! So he sent his arm off on its own to creep through Mousehammer's study window and steal a report card!" said Chris.

"Ha, I don't believe it!" said Sooz.

"That's what I said! But . . . But then . . ."

"What?" said Sooz, fascinated.

"Well, I went to see him, right? In his room. And I can't remember seeing his left hand at the time. He could have just had his sleeve pulled down, but I have to admit it didn't look like that. Then his eyes sort of glazed over. He said later that he was 'Guiding the hand with soul power.'"

"Soul power! Ooo, creepy—but cool! And I love the name, the Sinister Hand!" said Sooz, lapping it up.

"Heh, yeah, typical Dirk. Anyway, Mom called me away and I had to go. Later I saw Dirk—and he had a blank report card. But what was really weird was that his left arm looked kind of green and pale, and it was obviously hurting him. And there was a scar and everything! Just above the elbow. All red and nasty and swollen."

"Wow . . . ," said Sooz. "I mean . . . I mean . . . It couldn't be real could it?"

"Well . . . I don't know. He could have painted the scar on I suppose. He must have painted it on, right?"

"Yeah," said Sooz, trying to sound certain. "Of course he must have . . ."

"I mean, could he really have sent his hand off on its own with a magic spell? Could he?"

Part Three:
Trial and Terror

The PLAN

D irk felt it was time to take stock, to retrench and rethink. He wrote how he felt in his diary:

April GLOOM 21

Christopher finally came through on the Morti tickets. I really thought that the lead singer was really Gargon but my hopes were cruelly dashed. It was painfully obvious that the "band" was actually humans dressed in absurd rubber suits to make them look like demons. Gargon is not on this plane. There is no rescue mission. Nor will there ever be a rescue mission. Morti himself is nothing but a simple musician, even if the band does sound like one of the Nine Demon Choirs of the Netherworlds on too much coffee.

But I think I'll keep my Morti bag anyway—I just won't call it the Bag of Dread Gargon, Hewer of Limbs, anymore. It'll just be my Morti bag.

April GLOOM 27

Things are going from bad to worse. Today the Pure Guardians, Purejoie and Dr. Jack, took me to something called the Shoreham Air Show. It was a sobering experience. Human ingenuity is far greater than I had imagined. I'd read about their flying machines but nothing had prepared me for seeing them "in the flesh" as it were. The noise alone was enough to make my heart quail, let alone the heart of an Orc or a Goblin. And the weapon payload they are capable of! My Winged Nightgaunts wouldn't stand a chance. Even a score of Black Dragons couldn't take on a squadron of these "jet fighters."

I admit to a crushing sense of despair. I will have to revise all my plans. Whatever troops I could breed here or bring forth from other worlds will not be able to defeat their tanks and planes.

BLACK DRAGON VS F-18

It would take several lifetimes to create
the kind of numbers I would need. Can
it be that Hasdruban has truly defeated
me?

MAY DISMAY 3

I'd been toying with the idea of conquest
as a means to find the resources to
return home, but I now realize that even
conquering the local school is beyond me,
let alone the local town! Even if I
managed it somehow, my conquests would
be impossible to hold in the face of this
remarkable human technology. Either I
remain here and attempt to take power
through the usual channels, or I find
some other way to return home. Staying
here would mean waiting years to grow
up, and then becoming a senator and then
president, or joining the army, becoming
a general, and launching a military coup.
Either way it would take decades.

Gargon is not coming either. No, my
only certain hope is to open a portal
to the Darklands and return home, even
though it is fraught with danger. No
doubt by now Hasdruban and his fanatic

do-gooders will have had much time to
entrench their power.

I will have to come up with some kind
of spell or ritual for opening the way
between earth and the Darklands, as
the usual spell for this kind of thing—the
Ceremony of the Eclipse of the Gates of
the World—isn't possible on earth due
to the impossibility of finding the required
ingredients, such as the egg of a dragon.

Dirk began researching a way to travel between the
planes. He had to create a new spell or ceremony that
would do the job. He worked late for several nights
on his plans. In fact, he'd been working on it for so
long that he hadn't had much time to spend with his
lackeys, lickspittles, and worshippers, as he called the
Court in Exile, or "friends" as everyone else called
them. So, when he was ready, he summoned his closest courtiers: Chris, the "Mouth of Dirk"; Sooz, the
"Child of the Night"; and Sal Malik, the "Sports Lord,"
for a lunchtime meeting at school.

Dirk stood on a chair, to give himself extra height,
so that he could talk to them from a position of
authority. Or at least that's how it made him feel.

"I have made a decision!" he announced portentously, and paused to see what reaction he'd get. Chris

raised his eyes to heaven, as if to say, "Oh no, what's he up to this time?" which slightly irritated Dirk. Sooz smiled indulgently at him, if somewhat nervously, which pleased Dirk. She was so loyal. Sal just raised an eyebrow, like the excellent general he was, withholding judgment until he had all the facts.

"I am giving up my plans of world conquest. I am sorry, Sal. I know I promised you the position of Lord High Overseer of the Armies of Darkness, but that won't be possible now."

Sal shrugged his shoulders as if he wasn't bothered that much anyway. Christopher thought otherwise.

"Hold on a minute, you promised *me* the job of Lord High Overseer of the Armies of Darkness!" said Chris angrily, flicking a covert glance at Sooz as if he was worried what she might think of him if he was no longer going to be a Lord High Overseer.

"Ah," said Dirk, his eyes darting from side to side, as if he'd been caught in a lie, which in fact, he had. "I was going to tell you about that. Umm, you see, Sal would just make a much better general. And you, well, you're just perfect as the Mouth of Dirk . . ."

Dirk watched their faces. Sal looked pleased at this, even though it was obvious he thought of the Court in Exile as a game, and never really took it seriously. Still it was clear he liked the idea of being a great general, and he glanced over at Chris with a tinge of triumph in his eyes.

Chris looked a bit miffed though, so Dirk added, "In any case, the position of Mouth of Dirk is much more powerful, for you are much closer to the Throne of Skulls than a general, who will often be out campaigning with my Legions of Doom and Dread, and such."

This seemed to mollify Chris a bit, and he looked over at Sooz to see what she thought, and then over at Sal. But Sal put on an air of nonchalance, as if all this status stuff was beneath him anyway. Sooz looked on, somewhat disdainfully, as if she'd seen a hundred boys argue over stuff like this, and muttering under her breath something like, "Boys—they're all idiots."

In general, this was a constant problem—not so much that Sooz thought all boys were idiots (anyway, she had a point) but trying to balance the rivalries between his minions and servitors. Orcs and Goblins were easier to control because they responded so well to threats. These human children were much more complicated, and he couldn't use things like the Spell of Agonizing Obedience or the Vorpal Blade of Dismemberment to get things done. In fact, oddly, he noticed he didn't even want to use such spells on them anymore even if he could, because he didn't actually want to hurt them. It was almost as if he *cared* about them. Surely not, he thought to himself!

"Well, what *are* your plans then, now that you're

not going to bother with enslaving humanity?" said Sooz, breaking his train of thought.

"Ah, yes," replied Dirk. "I intend to open a portal between this plane and my own land, so I can get home. It will be dangerous—I'm not sure what will happen if I return. If I go back and remain in this body, without my powers, I will be easy meat for the White Wizard Hasdruban and his fanatic Paladins, Witch Hunters and other absurd do-gooders. If, however, I regain my original form and my powers, then it may be that I can get back to my tower in secret, rebuild my power and my legions, and take Hasdruban by surprise! My triumph will be complete, and my victory will be total! *Mwah, ha, ha!*"

His maniacal laugh echoed down the school corridors. It attracted the briefest of looks from passersby—the sound had become quite commonplace around the school these days and people were getting used to it.

"You're planning to leave us?" said Sooz.

She looked rather upset at the idea. Of course, thought Dirk, she can't bear to be parted from her Dark Master, Dirk the Magnificent, Lord of the Legions of Dread! She really was an excellent minion! He would have to reward her one of these days. Then Dirk's brow furrowed. He realized he didn't like to see her upset like this. That was confusing to him—you weren't really supposed to care about minions. So he tried explaining things, so she'd understand why he had to do it this way.

"Yes, I must try to get back. I'd take you with me, all of you, but there's no way of knowing if that's even possible. And if it is, it'd be dangerous—what hope would you have against the armies of the Commonwealth of Good Folk, their unstoppable Knights, Inquisitors, Magi, Elven bowmen and so on. No, it wouldn't be safe."

All three of them were looking at him oddly. It appeared they weren't buying the "it isn't safe" angle, so he decided to add some kind of general platitude—one of those lines that seemed to make these humans feel better.

"I couldn't bear to lose any of you. If you were killed over there, I'd feel just terrible. Guilty even." He smiled at that. He couldn't remember the last time he'd felt "guilt"—if ever, in fact.

"Don't worry," said Sal. "We won't be going with you, not because it's too dangerous, but because you won't be going anywhere either! It's just a game."

"Don't say that, Sal," said Sooz angrily. "You know he can't help it. Anyway, the point is that he wants to go. Alone. Without us . . ."

Dirk just smiled placidly. He'd learned how to deal with people not believing him. The important thing was that he believed in himself. And he did. Totally.

Chris said to Dirk, "So how are you going to open a portal between the worlds?"

"An interesting question," said Dirk. "There is a standard kind of spell for this, but it obviously wouldn't work here, so I've had to devise something entirely new. Do you remember my Cloak of Endless Night? Well, it's covered in Blood Glyphs of Power. Now, these Glyphs are powered, well, by blood, obviously, but also by interplanar sources of magical energy from beyond the stars, from beyond space and time, in fact. So, even though the Glyphs don't work here, the Cloak should still have a residual connection across the planes to the Darklands. I've written the new spell I've invented on a scroll, using the ancient runes of magic. All we have to do is seal the scroll, which means using my Ring of Power on the wax as the seal. The Ring that I gave Sooz." As he said this, he glanced over at her expectantly.

She grabbed the Ring on her finger protectively. "But I don't want to give up the Ring. I love it! It's the best present anyone's ever given me."

Dirk looked a bit taken aback for a moment, as if he hadn't expected her to care so much about it, or as if he'd expected her just to hand it over. Dirk thought for a moment. Hmm, he couldn't really just ask for it back. That would be unforgivably rude. He had gifted it to her, after all. So he said, "No, no, you can keep the

Ring. I just need you to use it to imprint my Great Seal on the wax, which will then be used to seal the magic scroll. We also need to get a small fire going, on which we burn various commonly available incenses and herbs. We lay the Cloak in the middle of the room, draw around it the symbol of the Five-Pointed Station of the Tetragram. I step onto the Cloak and then chant the spell, break the seal, and throw the scroll on the fire. The Cloak should dissolve into the very fabric of space and time itself, leaving an opening, a portal between the worlds for a brief moment, through which I can return home to the Darklands."

"Sounds simple enough," said Sal sarcastically. Then he asked, "What's this Cloak anyway, and where's it come from?"

"The Cloak of Endless Night and the Great Ring of Power are the only things that stayed with him when he fell to earth from the Darklands. Although they have lost their powers," said Sooz, almost like a litany, as she held up the Ring to show Sal. "See," she went on, "it has ancient runes carved on the inside."

"Indeed," agreed Dirk, "but for some reason my Helm of the Hosts of Hades, my Gauntlets of Ineluctable Destruction, and my Ebon Staff of Storms remained behind, or were perhaps sent to another plane entirely. Who knows?"

Sal shook his head disbelievingly. "You guys are

MY stuff

nuts! Still, it's creative, I'll give you that. You really should put it in a computer game or a book or something. Hey, I'd even read it myself, and the last two books I read were *The Hank Aaron Story* and *The Major League Almanac!*"

There was a pregnant pause. Sooz and Chris expected a "You dare question me, I, the Dark Lord?" moment, but Dirk chose to acknowledge Sal's comment as a compliment on his inventiveness rather than a judgment on his sanity. Dirk was learning to be diplomatic.

Dirk said, "Anyway, there is another problem. The location. We need a Pavilion of Dreams."

"A what?" said Chris.

"A Pavilion of Dreams. Names are important in magic. Places are important. You need the correctly named building in which to perform this kind of ritual. A place where dreams are made real by magic. Any ideas, anyone?" asked Dirk.

There was silence for a moment.

Then Sooz tentatively said, "I don't suppose we could build one somehow?"

"What? We're only kids, for goodness' sake," said Sal.

"Why do people say 'for goodness' sake'?" replied Dirk. "What's wrong with for evil's sake, for evil's sake? Anyway, it doesn't matter—building one *is* an option and I've been thinking about that. There's this spell I think would work even here, in this benighted place you ridiculous humans call earth. We could get the Skirrits of . . ."

"Wait a minute," interjected Sal. "What about the Players Pavilion?"

"The Players . . . ?" said Dirk, surprised by his suggestion, but also angered that he had dared to interrupt him. Just as he was about to launch into a tirade, Sal continued and what he said made Dirk forget his anger.

"Yeah, it's a real pavilion—it's got a sign over the door and everything."

Dirk's brow furrowed in thought. "Hmm, it might just do at that. It's always been called the Players Pavilion, right? Never been renamed?"

"Never—always been called that from the day it was built. You can read all about its history on that plaque inside," said Sal. "But, it's always been used for baseball, nothing else. Well, sports anyway. No crazy magic spells or anything, that's for sure!"

"That may not be a problem," said Dirk. "Baseball is a highly ritualized activity in itself, full of dreams of glory and prowess. In fact, I think the Players Pavilion will do fine. Thank you, Sal Malik, you have done well."

"A pleasure, my Lloyd of Dirkness," said Sal, smiling.

Dirk nodded and said, "We need to do this when there's no one else around."

"We?" said Sal.

"Absolutely," said Dirk. "I need my Inner Court, my closest attendants, my most trusted lieutenants to be there to help me."

Sooz and Chris exchanged a look. Chris raised his eyes and sighed resignedly. "Of course we'll be there."

"As your friends," added Sooz, though she didn't look too happy about it. It was the thought of losing Dirk that really got to her. It wouldn't happen though, she kept telling herself. The ritual wouldn't work. There was no such thing as magic, so it couldn't work, right?

Dirk looked over at Sal questioningly.

"Me? Oh all right, if you want," Sal said. "But you'd better help me draw up the best lineup for that game against Santa Ana Prep. They're best in the league, you know."

"Of course, of course—don't worry, the powers of their middle order batters are weak, and they lack skill in their bullpen. We can exploit these pitiful failings and crush them," said Dirk. "Now, down to business, as you humans like to say. Next Monday is a holiday—there'll be no one around then. We should perform the ritual in the pavilion at twelve noon, on Monday. The date and time is auspicious in terms of the

Conjunction of the Stars, and Monday was originally called Moon Day—moons have always been important in spells of this nature, both for interplanar travel and for dreams."

"That's all fine," said Chris, "but how are we going to get into the pavilion? It'll be locked. In fact, the whole school will be closed."

"Ah!" said Sal. "That's not a problem. I've got a set of keys. Special privilege and all that!"

"Perfect," said Dirk. "As for getting into the school—that's not too much of a problem either. When I was drawing up my plans for conquering the school, using Winged Nightgaunts, a platoon of Orcish Raiders, and a Goblin Horde, I examined the perimeter in detail. At the rear of the school, near the garden, there is a section of the wall where the top has crumbled somewhat. We ought to be able to climb over that quite easily, using a few of those old wooden crates they have lying around that area. We can pile them up like steps."

Dirk's enthusiasm was infectious. They were all getting into it. Coming up with solutions was fun. In fact, the whole idea seemed like fun. It was as if they were mighty wizards, performing a great spell that would change the world—though it was more of a game for the others than it was for Dirk. For him, of course, it was quite real.

Sooz said excitedly, "I've got a little gas cooker thing! And one of those Sterno cans they use on camping trips. We can use that to heat up the incense, and to burn the scroll."

"Excellent," said Dirk. "We shall meet at the top of Greenfield Lane at the eleventh hour of the morning, on Moon Day. The Child of the Night will bring the Ring of Power and the 'Unholy Flames of Calor'— don't forget to bring some matches as well, Sooz!— the Sports Lord will bring the Keys to the Pavilion of Dreams. I shall bring the Scroll of the Portal between the Worlds and the Ritual Incense and Chris . . . Errr."

Chris's brow knitted in irritation.

"Umm," spluttered Dirk. "Oh, of course, Chris can bring the wax. The sealing wax."

"The wax. I get to bring the wax. Great—I'll just bring a candle then?" complained Chris.

"Candle wax? Not really, it's not ideal," said Dirk.

"Actually, you can get sticks of wax in stationery stores. Little wax sealing kits with fake scrolls and stuff," said Sooz. "You should probably get red."

"Yes," added Dirk. "Red is good. The Sealing Wax of Enchantments. That's what we need, Chris. It's very important, really."

"Yeah, right." Chris folded his arms and scowled. He wanted to be a general, not just the mouthpiece of the Dark Lord, and he wanted a better job than "keeper of waxy stuff." Then he caught himself. He was worrying about a bunch of imaginary titles for positions that weren't even real, for goodness' sake. Or for evil's sake, rather! He chuckled to himself. He was taking being a lieutenant of the Lloyd of Dirkness a little too seriously.

"Okay, count me in," he said with a smile.

"Excellent!" said Dirk. "It is all settled then. Soon our plans shall come to full fruition!"

He threw back his head, putting his fingertips together in front of his chest, ready to give vent to his signature evil overlord's laugh, but he was taken by surprise when the others laughed along with him, mimicking the sound with their hands held together in the same way.

A chorus of *Mwah, ha, ha!* echoed around the school corridors, followed by general laughter as Sal, Chris, and Sooz cracked up at their spontaneous joke. Dirk looked down at them and smiled indulgently. He wasn't really sure what they were laughing about, but it seemed to make them happy, so why not? He needed them for the ritual.

Then the bell rang for the end of lunch, and they had to go to afternoon classes.

Later that evening, after supper, Dirk was sitting down with Chris in his room. They were playing a game called *Fantasy Wars* in multiplayer mode on the computer. This was a turn-based fantasy war game—Chris commanded the Human army, with Knights, Bowmen, Rangers, Eagle Riders, and various Heroes; Dirk commanded the Orcish army with Battle Orcs, Goblin archers, Trolls, Goblin airships, and so on.

Dirk had to put a lot of effort into getting Chris to play tonight. They'd already played this game on several occasions, and Dirk had utterly crushed Chris every time, so, understandably, Chris had gotten a bit bored with it all and was rather reluctant to play. But tonight, amazingly, Chris was getting the upper hand. And Chris was starting to get suspicious about it.

After one of his Royal Footmen units had stormed one of Dirk's Orcish strongholds rather too easily, Chris suddenly turned on Dirk and said angrily, "What's going on, Dirk? Are you deliberately letting me win?"

"Me? No, no! Of course not—I would never do that!" sputtered Dirk.

"Yes, you are," said Chris. "It's obvious. You're playing like a total idiot, for goodness' sake!"

"For evil's sake, you must mean! And no, you're just doing better than usual, really you are!" replied Dirk.

Chris threw the controls down in disgust. "Normally you're so good at this game it's like you were born to play it."

"Well . . . well, yes," said Dirk. "I was."

There was an uncomfortable silence for a second or two. Then Chris said, "What are you up to? What is it you want?"

"Oh, nothing, nothing," said Dirk airily.

"Come on, Dirk, I know you. What is it? Come on, out with it," said Chris.

Dirk sighed. He had underestimated Chris. In fact, he realized that he often did so. There was much more to Chris than met the eye. Chris looked at him expectantly.

"Well?" he said.

"Well, all right then, if you insist. You know my Ring of Power?" said Dirk.

"The one you gave Sooz? What about it?" said Chris.

Dirk paused for a moment. "You know I said Sooz could keep it? Umm, well, I was just saying that to keep her happy. In fact, I need it back," he said.

"Ah, I see! That's what this is all about. And I suppose you want me to ask her for you, is that it?" said Chris.

Dirk made a face and said, "Umm, no, not exactly. It would really hurt her feelings to ask for it back."

"Of course it would. She loves that ring!" replied Chris.

"Exactly. Instead, I want you to, er . . ." Dirk hesitated for a moment.

"Yes, what?" he said impatiently.

"I want you to steal it back for me," said Dirk, looking away innocently, as if it was all perfectly normal, and nothing to worry about.

There was a silence. Chris was annoyed with Dirk for springing this on him. For another thing, he didn't like the idea of stealing from Sooz. Dirk was putting him in a difficult position. Dirk was his friend—brother, even, if he was ever fully adopted—but Sooz was also his friend, and a good one too. And he liked her. A lot.

"You want me to steal it? Why?" said Chris rather tersely.

"I must have it back," said Dirk. "I need it for the ritual, but more important I must have it back if I am to return to the Darklands. Without it, I will be much diminished. No more than a minor Warlock or a Black Magus. Without the Ring I have little or no chance of defeating Hasdruban the Pure."

"Why did you give it to her in the first place then?!" asked Chris.

"It *was* rather rash of me. The Ring had lost all of its powers, as far as I could tell, so I had no use for it. But now it will be useful, whether it has power or not. Also, I liked her—she's so dark and vampire-y. If there's anyone in this ridiculous world of exams and hoodies who deserves to have it, it's her. It just seemed the right thing to do at the time. But in hindsight, a mistake—I see that now," said Dirk.

Chris paused for a moment, thinking, and then he asked, "Why can't you steal it back? You could use the Sinister Hand spell you said still worked on earth. Why do you need me?"

"A fair question," said Dirk, and he went on. "The Sinister Hand cannot handle relics of power. It would not be able to touch the Ring, and . . ."

"Oh, how convenient! More like there's no such thing as spells or magic!" Chris snapped back.

Dirk looked hurt at that. Of all the people on earth who he really wanted to believe him, Chris was one of the most important.

Chris knew this, so he always tried to humor Dirk whenever he could, just out of kindness, really. Chris felt a wave of remorse at his thoughtless words. Dirk really seemed to believe all this stuff and it wasn't really his fault that he did. In fact, sometimes Chris almost believed it too.

"Sorry," said Chris. "Sorry." Chris tried to think a bit like Dirk. He said, "Right then, the Sinister Hand is a minor magic, an enchantment that is not powerful enough to cope with the mighty sorceries that bind great relics like the Ring of Power, is that it?"

"Precisely!" said Dirk enthusiastically. "You've got

it exactly, Chris! You're learning—perhaps one day you will be able to take up the study of Wizardry!"

Chris smiled.

Then Dirk said, "But actually, there is another much more mundane reason I want you to steal the Ring. Opportunity. And swimming practice."

"Swimming practice?" said Chris.

"Indeed," replied Dirk. "You know Sooz goes swimming every Thursday night after school. And she goes straight from school, so she gives you her AngelBile bag to drop off at her place for her."

"Yeah," said Chris, not sure where this was going.

"And she can't wear jewelry in the swimming pool, so she leaves it all in her bag—the rings, bracelets for ankle and wrist, the toe rings, earrings, everything . . . You see?"

"Ah, of course!" said Chris. "The perfect opportunity!"

"Right," said Dirk. "You don't even have to do anything, as she's just going to give you the Ring anyway. Later, she'll ask about it, but you just deny everything, and she'll just think she lost it before she put it in the bag. It's so much easier than spells and stuff!"

There was another reason, of course, but Dirk wasn't going to mention it to Chris. The other reason was that Dirk was always trying to get other people to do things for him. That was one of the things that made a Dark Lord a Dark Lord. What was the point of having lackeys, underlings, lickspittles, and minions if you didn't get them to do things for you?! No, it was better that his lieutenant did it for him—that was how evil overlords got things done.

Chris shook his head admiringly. "You are smart, I'll give you that, Dirk!" he said.

"So, you'll do it then?" asked Dirk. "I need it in time for the ritual on Monday."

Chris paused for a moment, thinking. Then he sighed, and said, "All right, I'll do it, but I'm not going to steal for you ever again, Dirk, and that's final!"

"Of course, of course," said Dirk. "Never again. Never!"

Dirk was smiling broadly. He put his hands in front of his chest, joined them at the fingertips, and said, "The Ring shall soon be mine! *Mwah, ha, ha!*"

Chris had to laugh at that and the mood lightened. Later, when Dirk had gone to write in his diary, Chris stared at the ceiling in thought. One of the reasons why Sooz gave him the bag to take home for her was so that it couldn't be stolen while she was swimming. She was putting her stuff into his hands for safekeeping. She trusted him. Today was a Monday—three days before her swimming practice. They had a week. He reached for his cell phone and called Sooz . . .

As Christopher called Sooz on his phone, Dirk sat

at the table in his room, working on his diary. He'd been feeling relatively pleased with the way things were going, except for those accursed reports and the recurring nightmare that always featured some kind of white beast hunting him down. He'd found an odd newspaper story that was most intriguing, so he cut it up and pasted it into his diary. Could it be this that he was dreaming of?

Meanwhile, elsewhere in Whiteshields . . .

The Wendle Herald

Local News

The White Lynx of Whiteshields

Most of you may recall the so-called sightings of the Whiteshields puma, said to be a black cougar, back in the 70s and 80s. Well, now we have the white lynx, or possibly the snow leopard. Over 43 sightings have been reported in the Whiteshields area in the last two weeks— and all the reports are the same. A large white cat, but big, at least 4 feet in length and unusual looking—like a lynx or a snow leopard or possibly an albino puma. No livestock has been hurt but the police are asking people to be careful, just in case. Detective Inspector Carwen

Ma Baker, a gray-haired, stooped, shriveled old lady, rested her tired bones on a bench and threw bread to a pair of sparrows. One of them landed close to a small black oil slick in an empty parking spot. It pecked at it and froze, wobbling on its little legs for a moment before falling head first into the scummy, oily blackness.

Then it stood back up again . . . But it seemed bigger than before, and its feathers were as black as night, covered with a film of slime. It looked more like a crow than a sparrow. A black storm crow with bloodred eyes. It gave a caw of malignant rage and took to the air before swooping down and attacking its one-time mate. Ma Baker could only look on in astonished amazement.

THE PAVILION
OF DREAMS

May DISMAY 1⁹

Today Sooz insisted on taking me to see one of her favorite places. I expected it to be something a typical twelve-year-old human girl-child would like, or something "girlie" as Christopher would say, but in fact it sounded quite interesting, or so I thought. Her favorite place turns out to be in the nearby town of Wendle, and it's a witches museum.

Apparently these were human women burned at the stake for their crimes, hundreds of years ago, but they weren't what I'd call witches. Little black capes, silly crooked hats, long warty noses. And broomsticks, for evil's sake! What, they clean you to death? "Surrender now, or

I will sweep your front room!" Ha! And
I told Sooz so—"You should see the
witches we have back in the Darklands!
The Crow Witch, the Black Hag, the
Accursed Crone, Our Lady of Shadows,
the Withered One of a Hundred Hexes, to
mention but a few. Now they're witches!"
I said.

This made Sooz really angry—"Well,
if the Darklands are so good, why don't
you go back home then? Go off with one
of your witches, if they're so much better,
and leave us alone!"

"I am trying to get home," I said. That
seemed to make her even angrier, and
she stomped off in a huff. Didn't talk to
me for days. I'll never understand these
humans, especially the females.

May DISMAY 21, YEAR OF OUR LORD DIRK: 1

Mr. Grousammer, the principal, makes
such efforts to annoy me that I suspect
he may be Hasdruban the Pure under the
guise of a Mask of Flesh spell. The only
way to know for sure would be to affix
the stings of 1,001 killer bees from his jaw

to his neck, and then pull. However, the
plan is not without difficulty. Also, if
I'm wrong, there is a serious risk of
detention. Again.

It was Friday, the last day at school before the day off.
Sooz found Dirk during morning break and took him
to one side for a private word. She seemed quite upset
about something.

"Dirk, I'm sorry. I've lost the ring you gave me!"
she said, somewhat guiltily.

"Oh dear, I'm sorry to hear that, Child of the
Night!" said Dirk, trying to appear surprised. In fact,
he had the Ring in his pocket and he was fiddling with
it even as they spoke. Chris had given it to him last
night after supper.

"Somehow I lost it during swimming practice. I've
searched the locker room but . . . nothing. I'm really
sorry!"

"Don't worry about it," said Dirk, as his brow furrowed. Something didn't feel quite right. He was expecting Sooz to be a lot more upset about it, but she didn't
seem *that* bothered. Hadn't she said it was the best present he'd ever given her, the best present *anyone* had ever
given her?

"What about the ritual on Monday?" asked Sooz.
"Can you do it without the ring?"

"Oh yes, of course. I have other seals. Don't worry about it, my little Vampire!" said Dirk, almost affectionately.

"Oh, okay then," said Sooz airily. "I'm off now—English with Battle Axe," and she raised her eyes to heaven. Dirk groaned in sympathy as she walked away. She waved at him over her shoulder.

Dirk stood there, puzzled. She didn't need to rush off like that. Classes didn't start for a good ten minutes. Could Sooz be losing interest in him? Didn't she care anymore? He'd expected a few more tears, or something. He shrugged. Perhaps he'd just misread the whole situation. Maybe it wasn't that important to her after all. Maybe it was just because it was the last day before the long weekend, and she was in too good a mood to cry about it? Yes, that must be it, he thought. Holidays always seem to make human children happy . . . Or was something else going on?

Dirk took the Ring out and put it on his finger, turning it ruminatively. It felt dull, lifeless. Empty and powerless. (But then it had always felt like that ever since he had come to this absurd place these ridiculous humans called home.) When he got back to the Darklands, he was sure the Ring would be filled with dark energy again, and glow once more with its eerie black light. Only a few more days to go. Home to the Iron Tower, to his Gates of Doom, and his Throne of Skulls! There would be much to do, and he would have to keep it all secret, to hide in the shadows until he had rebuilt his power, assuming his old form would return as well. Imagine if he remained in this body! But he tried not to think about it. That was too awful to contemplate. His brow furrowed. He realized with surprise that he would miss some things here in Whiteshields. He would miss Sooz. He would miss Chris. Even Mrs. Purejoie. A little bit.

His thoughts were interrupted by Chris and Sal.

"Yo, Dark Lord," said Sal in greeting.

"Sports Lord," said Dirk, acknowledging his greeting with a regal nod of the head.

"I've got the sealing wax," said Chris, holding up a thick, deep-red-colored stick of wax. "All ready for Monday."

"Excellent!" said Dirk. "All is ready! Soon I shall be free of this accursed plane! The Darklands await my triumphant return! *Mwah, ha, ha!*"

Chris and Sal glanced at each other and smiled. Everyone was in a good mood today—either because a holiday was coming up or they believed they were going home to another land, on another plane, in another universe. Mostly though, it was because of the holiday.

Soon Monday dawned, a clear, sunny day with an almost cloudless sky. A beautiful day. At the eleventh hour, Chris, Sooz, Sal, and Dirk met at the top of Greenfield Lane. Sooz had a small gas burner, a Sterno can, and a big box of kitchen matches. Chris had his sealing wax, Sal had the keys to the pavilion, and Dirk had the scroll and the incense.

"Welcome, my Magi!" said Dirk. "Today a great sorcery will be wrought! We shall open a magic portal between two worlds, a thing never before done on earth! Well, not since Hasdruban sent me here in the first place that is, but that's neither here nor there!"

Sal, Sooz, and Chris smiled indulgently.

"Well, let's get on with it then," said Sooz, and they ambled down the lane. Greenfield Lane was long and leafy. It was a hot day. Birds sang in the trees, and unseen creatures rustled in the hedgerows as they passed. It was earth, however, so the "unseen creatures" tended to be things like shrews, hedgehogs, squirrels, and rabbits, rather than skulking Goblins, dark Elves, or the undead. More's the pity, Dirk thought to himself.

After a few hundred yards, the lane dipped into a low depression, rising up on the other side to the school's backyard and the garden.

Sal was just ahead of the group when he crested the top of the rise. He pulled up short and ducked down out of sight, hugging the wall. He gestured for the rest to do the same by holding his fist up, as if this was some kind of army patrol. Chris made a face at Sooz, holding his own fist up in mockery of Sal, and shaking

MY KIND OF LEDGE

his head. "We're not in the army, are we?" he whispered, raising his eyes to heaven.

Sooz shrugged and whispered back, "I think he's sweet." Chris shook his head in mock disgust.

"He's very good-looking too," she added.

Chris grimaced. For some reason, that really annoyed him, and he turned away from her grumpily. Sooz smiled. She'd gotten the reaction she wanted. She looked at Dirk, to see his reaction, but he was just looking over at Sal, and shushing her and Chris into silence with his hands. Sooz scowled. Why didn't Dirk take more notice of her? Didn't he care that she might like Sal more than him? Chris seemed to care about it.

Sal poked his head up over the rise for another quick look to confirm what it was that had spooked him. He turned, and hissed in a harsh whisper, "It's Mousehammer!"

It was Principal Grousammer. He was there working on his garden, tending his vegetables. He was sure to see them if they tried to get over the school wall.

"Curses!" said Dirk. "A thousand curses on the heads of little golden-eyed goody-two-shoes Elf children, may their hearts be ripped out and sacrificed to the Dark Gods of Chaos!" he muttered.

They crouched out of sight. The sun beat down. All was quiet, save for birdsong, and the sound of Grousammer's trowel, clinking against the occasional pebble as he worked the soil. Dirk examined the position of the sun. He looked at Chris and nodded toward Chris's arm. Chris realized what he meant and checked his wristwatch.

"Eleven twenty," he whispered.

Dirk gnawed on his lower lip. The ceremony had to be performed at twelve noon. Sooz and Chris were looking at him expectantly. He realized they were waiting for him to come up with something. Well, he knew what to do. He called the group together in a huddle.

"I knew it was a possibility that Grousammer would be working on his garden—you must know your enemy, as the saying goes. I have planned for this," said Dirk.

With that, Dirk took something out of his pocket.

"A grenade? That's a grenade!" said Sal in a shocked whisper.

"You're going to blow him up?" hissed Sooz, equally shocked.

"You can't kill him, Dirk, for goodness' sake!" said Chris.

Dirk raised his eyes and made a face.

"I've told you already, Chris, that should be for evil's sake. And no, of course not, you idiots! It's not a real grenade—well, it doesn't have any explosives in it, put it that way."

Chris and Sooz just blinked at him, nonplussed.

"Where did you get it?" asked Sal in a whisper.

"I made it in science class—cost me a few detentions, in fact. Took ages to make it look this old. Here you are, Sal, this is your province, I believe," said Dirk and he handed the grenade to Sal.

Sal took it. Looked at it. Looked up at Dirk.

"Throw it! Like a baseball. Just behind Grousammer. He'll think he's dug up an old grenade or something. He'll have to leave and call the police—unexploded bomb and all that."

"Oh," said Sal. Then he grinned. Sooz and Chris chuckled. This was going to be fun! Sal poked his head up to see what Grousammer was up to. When the moment was right, he lobbed it into the garden. It landed with a chink. Sal ducked down back out of sight. Perfect throw, he signaled to Dirk, making a little circle with thumb and forefinger.

A few moments passed in silence. Suddenly Grousammer shouted at the top of his voice: "Argh! A grenade!" They heard the sound of him hitting the ground, as he dove for cover.

They all clapped their hands over their mouths to stop themselves from laughing out loud. They began to shake and shudder, seized by uncontrollable giggling.

"Oh, you idiot," they heard Grousammer saying to himself. "It's probably been here for ages by the look of it. Pull yourself together."

Then they heard him standing up. "Better go and call the police," he muttered and began to walk back toward the school. The plan was working perfectly.

Dirk managed to control his laughter. He said, "He might be back soon. Sal, can you distract him, delay him a little longer? You're supposed to be seeing him about a batting cage anyway, aren't you?"

"Yeah, I'm supposed to be seeing him tomorrow. I could go after him," offered Sal. "Just walk past as if by chance and suggest we talk about it now."

"That would be most useful," said Dirk.

"But don't you want to see the ritual?" said Sooz.

"Yeah," added Chris in a low voice. "What if Dirk actually does open a portal between the worlds?"

Sooz's brow furrowed. She didn't like the idea of Dirk leaving, but on the other hand, she *knew* the "spell" wouldn't work. Well, she was fairly certain anyway. As was Chris, surely. Sal, was totally certain, though.

"Yeah, right. There ain't gonna be no portal opening, dudes! More like Dirk is some twentieth-level magic-user class thing or whatever, Sooz is some kind of Vampire type character, Chris is a twelfth-level blah in whatever weirdo, nerdy live-action, role-playing game you guys are into."

"I guess so," said Sooz.

"I suppose that's one way of looking at it," added Chris.

But Dirk glared at Sal and said, "Twentieth-level magus? A mere twentieth-level human magus! I am at least a fiftieth-level Dark Lord, for evil's sake. And I . . ." Dirk's voice was beginning to rise.

Chris put his finger to his lips to warn him to keep quiet, in case Grousammer could still hear him. Dirk got ahold of himself.

"Bah, it is not a game, I tell you!" he hissed.

"Sure, whatever," said Sal. "Anyway, look, I'm not into those sorts of games, but fine if you are. Here are the keys to the pavilion. Just give 'em back to me tomorrow morning, okay?"

He handed the keys to Dirk, who accepted them rather ungraciously. Dirk realized he was being unnecessarily rude so he bowed and whispered, "Excellent, Sports Lord Malik! I, the Great Dirk, thank you for your tribute and your superb throwing skills!"

Sal shook his head like Dirk was nuts, but he couldn't stop himself from chuckling a little and grinning from ear to ear. "Yeah, no prob, Your Dirkness. Just don't tell anyone I gave you those keys! I'd lose my place as captain—not to mention getting a ton of detentions."

"Don't worry, we'll keep it quiet," said Chris.

"And I shall draw up an unbeatable plan to crush Santa Ana Prep!" added Dirk.

"Cool. Okay then, good luck—I'll see you later," said Sal.

"Perhaps not," replied Dirk, "but thank you for your excellent services, Sal Malik!"

With that, Sal nodded and walked over to the garden. They could see him running after Grousammer, and after a few moments both of them disappeared out of sight.

Sooz, Chris, and Dirk stood up and made their way to the low wall at the back of the school. Using the wooden crates from the garden, they climbed over the wall with ease, and made their way to the baseball field, where the pavilion stood silently, as if waiting for them.

They trooped inside and began to prepare for the ritual. With a piece of chalk, Dirk carefully drew the symbol of the Five-Pointed Station of the Tetragram on the wood floor. Nearby, Sooz set up the gas burner, and lit it with a match. She put the Sterno can on the flame. Chris stood by with the sealing wax, feeling a little left out. "Keeper of the Sealing Wax," "he who melts the Wax," "Wax-bearer" didn't really have the ring of greatness to it, now did it? he thought to himself.

Dirk laid his Cloak of Endless Night on the ground. It seemed to fill the space in the Five-Pointed Station of the Tetragram almost perfectly, as if it knew where to go. He then sprinkled some herbs (mostly ordinary stuff— peppercorns, rosemary, bay leaves, bergamot oil, and the like) into the Sterno can on the gas cooker. Quickly it began to smoke, giving off a lovely fresh smell.

He then took out the scroll, and nodded at Chris who stuck the wax into the gas fire. It melted rapidly, and they sealed the scroll. With his back to Sooz, so she couldn't see, Dirk took out the Ring and imprinted the seal part of it into the soft wax, leaving his mark. The Ring was supposed to be lost, after all. But Sooz and Chris exchanged a look behind Dirk's back as if they knew exactly what was going on.

Then Dirk began to chant. A weird chant—some kind of strange language Chris and Sooz had never heard before. The inside of the pavilion seemed to go strangely quiet. The hairs stood up on the back of Sooz's and Chris's necks. They looked at each other again, but this time they were a little scared. The chanting really seemed magical. And it was disturbing, weirdly unpleasant.

Was it her imagination, or did the air seem to be wavering above the cloak, like a heat-haze mirage, thought Sooz. She looked over at Chris. He was staring at the same patch of air. He could see it too! This couldn't be real could it? Surely it couldn't?

Then Dirk stopped the weird chant. By now, the soft wax seal had hardened. He snapped it, crying out some word or command in a language that sounded like it was not meant for the human tongue. Then he lit the scroll and plunged it into the burning incense. The whole thing burst into a thin column of green flame, as if incense, scroll, and wax had been instantly consumed in a flash of magical fire! Dirk turned and stepped onto the Cloak.

"Good-bye, my lieutenants, good-bye!" he said.

Chris and Sooz were astonished. Could he really be leaving them? They looked at each other desperately.

But nothing happened. Nothing. The gas burner hissed on. The Cloak lay there, unmoving. Dirk looked puzzled and frustrated. He jumped up and down on the Cloak. He picked it up, wrapped it around him, and rechanted the spell. But nothing happened. Nothing seemed to work.

"What's going on? Why isn't it working?" he shouted. Then he raised his arms up, spreading the Cloak wide, and cried out to the heavens, "Why, why? Am I cursed to remain forever trapped on this plane, weak and powerless for all time?"

Sooz looked relieved though, and she stepped over, put her arm around Dirk, and said, "You'll always have me, Dirk. And I'm glad it didn't work. I didn't want you to go in the first place."

Amazingly, he didn't seem to mind this closeness, this intrusion—in fact Dirk rested his head on her shoulder, taking comfort in her sympathy, and said, "Thank you Sooz, thank you. I would have missed you too." Sooz smiled happily.

Chris looked relieved too, but perhaps for other reasons. He'd begun to think that maybe Dirk really was from another world, and that would have been so incredible, so extraordinarily mind-blowing, he wasn't sure that he could have handled it. But now he realized it was all just an elaborate game after all, and Dirk was making it up. All this magic stuff was just in their own minds. And that was so much easier to deal with.

"I'm sorry, Dirk," said Christopher. "Maybe, you know . . . Maybe it's, you know . . . Maybe this was just taking it too far. Maybe you're not really a Dark Lord and all that."

Dirk straightened up, his face a mask of anger. "How dare you question me? Don't you know who I am? I am the Dark Lord! Master of the Legions of Dread and Sorcerer Supreme! My home is the Iron Tower of Despair, beyond the Plains of Desolation!"

In his anger, he kicked out at the pot of incense and ashes, sending the little gas burner flying. It slammed into the wall, coming to rest against the old wooden timbers of the pavilion.

"Whoa, don't worry! Small fire, small problem," said Chris, as he darted forward to turn off the gas burner.

But then, without warning, the old timbers burst into flame, and the fire began to spread fast, licking along the old planks as if they were coated in gasoline!

"What the . . . ! Get out of here, now!" shouted Christopher at the top of his voice, and he ran for the doorway with Sooz right behind him.

Dirk paused for a moment, mesmerized by the flames, staring at them as they grew, a fascinated smile spreading across his features. The reddish glow lit up his face and eyes, and, just then, for a moment Dirk really looked like a Dark Lord, standing over some burning city his Orcish legions had just sacked, watching the flaming inferno and laughing in wild triumph.

"Come on, Dirk," screamed Sooz. "We've got to get out of here!"

Dirk, shocked out of his reverie, turned and sprinted for the door.

When they burst out into the afternoon sunlight, they paused for a moment, unsure what to do next, a rising sense of panic overwhelming them. Had they just set fire to the Players Pavilion? This was bad! Already, flames were belching out of the windows and a whirling genie of black smoke was spiraling upward.

Dirk was gazing at the burning pavilion, fascinated by the flames. He appeared distracted, not his usual self.

"Are you all right, Dirk?" said Sooz.

Dirk looked over at her. His face shocked her. Instead of the usual mischievous grin, the regal arrogance, the confident self-belief, there was only misery, grief, despair, and hopelessness.

"I really thought that would work . . . ," he muttered, almost to himself.

"Don't worry, I'm sure we can try again," said Chris.

"But right now we really need to get moving. What should we do, Dirk?"

"What?" Dirk said. "What?"

"What do we do, Dirk? What do we do?" asked Chris.

"Oh, yes, of course," said Dirk. He pulled himself together. "We must split up. Go and do something other people can check. You know, get an alibi. Like asking your mom if you can go to the movies, Sooz, something like that. We'll meet later tonight, at the Purejoies. There we'll draw up a plan, and make sure our stories match. Denial, denial, denial! I'll see you later, but for now, I must be alone." With that, Dirk dashed off toward the garden.

"Oh, God, we're in for it now," said Sooz. Chris looked at her, his panic-stricken face sick with worry. But then he pulled himself together.

"I guess he's right," said Chris. "Maybe we can get away with it. Dirk will come up with something. If anyone can, he can."

"Yeah, Dirk'll fix it," said Sooz. That thought calmed them down a little.

"Let's go, before the police and the fire department get here. I'll see you later, Sooz," said Chris, and he headed off after Dirk.

Sooz set out after him. Behind them, the pavilion roared with flames. As they were nearing the low wall by the garden, she saw Chris ducking down out of sight behind a bush.

Suddenly Grousammer came over the wall, running straight toward the pavilion, his face agog.

He drew up short when he saw Sooz, and shouted, "Susan Black! You've got to get away from here! Quick, this way . . ."

Grousammer was trying to save her. Sooz waved her hand in acknowledgment.

Grousammer looked at her hand and his eyes narrowed in suspicious anger. Sooz followed his gaze. Her hand was closed around a big box of kitchen matches . . .

The TROUBLE with SOOz

Sooz stood despondently in Grousammer's office. She was in big trouble this time! He had taken her to his office, told her in no uncertain terms to wait there, and then rushed off to deal with the fire department, the police, and the bomb squad. As she stood there, worrying about what was going to happen, she noticed a book on Grousammer's desk. It looked like his diary. She couldn't help herself . . . With a guilty backward glance at the door, she leaned over, turned the diary to face her, and opened it.

The Diary of Hercules Grousammer

A RECORD OF THE EXPLOITS OF THE GREAT ~~EXPLORER~~ ~~MOUNTAINEER,~~ ~~LEGAL MIND OF THE CENTURY~~ . . . TEACHER
One day, this will constitute the memoirs of the greatest school principal ever!

Sooz grinned—Hercules, what a name! Wait till she told Dirk. She flipped through a few pages near the end at random.

May 8

I took a nap in the school garden today. I woke up an hour or so later with several painful bee stings. Can't understand how getting stung like that didn't wake me up! What was most odd was that the bee stings formed a perfect circle around my jawline and neck.

May 9

I don't know why, but I just get the feeling that that little reprobate Dirk Lloyd had something to do with that bee sting episode. If I could find a way of expelling the boy I would. Oh, for a return to corporal punishment!

May 23

One of the little horrors managed to steal some school report cards, and wrote up a set of reports on the teachers, and then passed them around to all the children in the playground. I've attached a copy, as evidence should I ever find the culprit. And when I find out who did it, they shall be punished severely! We must maintain the proper respect and

Whiteshields School Report: Grousammer, Mousehammer,

Teacher: The Pupils

~~SCIENCE~~ Overall	Needs regular help to ensure progress at times	Making progress with some help overall	Making satisfactory progress overall	Making good progress	Achieves a consistently high standard overall
KNOWLEDGE AND ITS APPLICATION	✓				
UNDERSTANDING & CARRYING OUT INVESTIGATIONS	✓				
INTERPRETING RESULTS & DRAWING CONCLUSIONS	✓				
RECORDING & PRESENTATION OF WORK	✓				

EFFORT	Needs to improve ✓	Varies	Satisfactory	Good	Very good	Excellent

~~Teacher's~~ comment:
Pupils'

Grousammer is one of the worst principals we have ever come
across. He is a cruel, despotic tyrant, arbitrary, capricious, and
fundamentally flawed in every way that it is possible to be flawed in.
His only purpose seems to be to make history lessons bearable—
by playing the game of Guess the Grousammer. This involves going
back through history and finding all the thieves, murderers, serial
killers, dictators, madmen, tyrants, despots, and general scum of
humanity and seeing how similar they are to Grousammer. Especially
those with silly beards. To help with his waxy, puttylike complexion
and bloodshot, beady stare, we recommend that during the holidays
he should try some healthy outdoor activities such as wind-surfing,
ideally with a plastic board on a lake of boiling lava.

deference due to us teachers! I already have my
suspicions . . . If ever they did a book or a movie on
the childhood of one of those Bond villains, like
Dr. No or Blofeld, or a supervillain like that
preposterous Dr. Doom, they'd not be far off the
mark with that Dirk Lloyd boy. If ever a boy was
going to grow up to be such a criminal mastermind
it's him. Hmm—"it is he," I should say. Don't want
to lose points for poor English, ha ha.

May 25

The superintendent trapped me again after the
school board meetings. He's a persistent you-
know-what, I'll give him that. Insists on seeing the
receipts for the Players Pavilion fireproofing job. I
don't think I can delay him much longer, blast it.
I'll have to think of something.

That last entry was intriguing. What could it mean?
She'd have to tell Dirk about that as well. Suddenly
Sooz heard footsteps outside the door. She quickly
flipped the diary shut, and put it back in its place.
Grousammer stomped into the room, glaring at her.
He glanced at his diary, and then up at Sooz suspi-
ciously. He sat down angrily, snatched it up, and put it
away in the drawer of his desk.

Sooz endured a lecture on the responsibilities
and duties of a young girl in the modern world,

how disappointed he and all the staff were with her, how disappointed her mother would be, how black eyeliner and a lip-piercing were not looks that the school wanted to encourage, and how serious a matter it was to burn down the school pavilion.

"But it wasn't me," protested Sooz weakly. She was feeling very intimidated by the whole thing and was trying to hold down a rising sense of fear and panic, and all she could manage was a rather feeble protest. Grousammer chewed her head off anyway.

"Oh please, don't waste my time with lying, Susan Black! I caught you running from the conflagration with a box of matches in your hand!"

"But, but—"

"But nothing, Miss Black! This is a serious matter. I am considering calling the police. They'd arrest you for arson, for goodness' sake—a serious matter! You could be expelled from school, even charged!" shrieked Grousammer, spittle flying from his mouth, his lips drawn back in an angry snarl.

Sooz sniveled piteously, but that only seemed to make Grousammer angrier.

"And you didn't even give a second thought to what this will do to the reputation of the school! We'll have the superintendent all over us now, you little idiot!" howled Grousammer, his shrieking rage taking him over completely.

Sooz stepped back. Grousammer's lost it, she thought to herself. But then his words began to sink in. Sooz held back tears. It was so unfair that he wouldn't let her get a word in. And what will her mother think, and all her friends? The thought of it made her feel so ashamed. And it wasn't even her fault. She couldn't control it anymore, tears rolling down her face as she began to cry.

"It's too late for tears now, Miss Black," said Grousammer cruelly, almost as if he was enjoying this.

"But," sniveled Sooz, staring at the floor. "But . . . it was an accident. It was only a little fire, and the whole thing went up so fast! It shouldn't have burned up like that. I don't know what happened, it was just my camping stove, a little thing . . ." Sooz looked up.

Grousammer had fallen silent, a hand up at his beard, slowly stroking it thoughtfully. He flicked his eyes from side to side shiftily. Then his whole demeanor changed.

"Er, yes, well. Yes, it does sound like an unfortunate accident," he said, handing Sooz a handkerchief from his jacket pocket.

Sooz wiped her tears away with the handkerchief. She knew something had changed, but wasn't quite sure what. Even so, she was going to go along with it. Sniffing, she said, "Oh, it *was*, Mouseham . . . I mean, Mr. Grousammer. It was an accident, really."

Grousammer scowled. He hated his nickname, and any use of it within range of his hearing would normally bring instant detention, but he seemed strangely distracted at the moment.

Sooz thought furiously. The whole thing was Dirk's fault. And Grousammer had been horrible to her. She hated him! If only Dirk really was a Dark Lord instead of just a weird kid. Though that was one of the things she loved about Dirk—he was strange. The strangest Goth ever! The thought of him cheered her up a little. But what should she do? Tell the truth and tell Mousehammer it was Dirk? But would he believe her—Dirk and Christopher weren't even spotted anywhere near the pavilion, and she had been carrying the matches. By now, knowing Dirk, he probably had a cast-iron alibi anyway. Should she take the rap for Dirk? Maybe he'd spend more time with her if she did. What to do? Grousammer wasn't quite himself either—and she didn't know why.

Grousammer scowled some more. He drummed his fingers on the desk, deep in thought, the other hand scratched at his beard. Sooz raised an eyebrow. What was the crazy old monster up to, she wondered.

"What were you doing there, anyway?" he growled.

Sooz decided to make it up as she went along. "I was just playing."

"Playing? At your age? What do you mean?" snarled Grousammer.

"Well, you know, errr—camping. I was practicing

camping. Girl Scouts. I took my gas cooker. Cooked up some hot dogs. But then I knocked it over," said Sooz. She was getting ahold of herself now.

"I see," said Grousammer, in a tone of voice that meant he didn't see, and he didn't believe.

Undeterred, Sooz pressed on—I might as well keep going, she thought, and said, "Yeah, that's it. And the whole place went up. In seconds. We . . . I mean, *I* was lucky to get out alive!"

"Ah, yes, well. Umm, most unfortunate," sputtered Grousammer, drumming his fingers even more feverishly on his desk.

"I mean, you saw it when you got there. I'd only just got out—it went up so fast!" she added.

Grousammer raised his eyes. Then he sighed and said, "Yes, yes. Well, we'll see. I think for now we'll assume you're telling the truth. The fire department will investigate no doubt . . ." Grousammer trailed off.

Sooz could have sworn she noticed a look of panic in his eyes. What was going on?

Then he said, "Umm, I'll have to suspend you for a few days, anyway. Can't have people burning down the pavilion—even by accident—and getting away with it scot-free, you know. But if the, umm, investigation confirms what you're saying, then you can come back to school. If not, well, I may still pass the matter on to the police."

"Yes, sir," said Sooz meekly. She wasn't going to rock the boat—so far just getting away with a suspension was pretty good, and she'd got Chris and Dirk off the hook. They'd owe her for that.

"Well, off you go then, Miss Black. I suggest you go home immediately. In the meantime, I'll call your mother and tell her what happened, and what my decision is."

Sooz nodded. She knew he'd be telling her at some point—Mom wouldn't be pleased, but if Grousammer accepted her story, Mom would too. Sooz didn't need any encouragement to get out of there, so she turned and left. As she walked out the door, she noticed she still had Grousammer's handkerchief in her hand. It was monogrammed, with the letters HG etched in gold on one corner. Hercules . . . It took all her willpower to stop herself from sniggering out loud—that certainly wouldn't have gone over well! She hurried away, handkerchief in hand, half laughing, half fearful of what the future would hold.

Later that evening, after her mother had reamed her out, and grounded her for a whole week, Christopher called.

"Hi, Sooz, whatcha doing?"

"Playing *Realm of Shadows*."

"What, that worthless online role-playing game?"

"Yeah, it's cool."

"Nah, it stinks! Don't know why you don't play *Battlecraft* with me and Dirk."

"Well, *Realm of Shadows* doesn't look as good, and it's not nearly as big, but it's free. It's also got a Nightwalker character class, which is really, really cool. Oh, and did I say it was free? You know, *free*!"

"Yeah, whatever. I've seen it and it's the worst."

"Yeah, whatever to you too, fudge boy. I like it, so forget you. Anyway, is that why you called—to diss my favorite game?"

"Er, no, no. Sorry. I . . . Look, Sooz, did Mousehammer get you?"

"Yeah, he did."

"Oh my God! What did you say?"

"Well, I said it was just me. You two are off the hook."

"Wow!" There were a few moments of silence as Christopher digested this information. Then, "Jeez, thanks, Sooz, thanks a lot . . . But doesn't that mean, you know, the police and stuff?"

"Maybe."

"Look, you don't have to do that, Sooz. It's not fair. We'll 'fess up."

"No, it's all right. I said it was an accident. Just me, cooking some hot dogs."

"Hot dogs! You're kidding. You're not telling me the old vulture believed that, are you?"

"Yeah, he did, sort of. For now, anyway."

"What did he do then? Didn't he get the police in?"

"Well, no, Mousehammer just suspended me. It was weird. Like he didn't want too much fuss made over it all."

"What? Why?"

"Don't know—there's something going on. He's worried about something. Except, he did say he might still tell the police. Depends what happens with the fire investigation. Anyway, where's Dirk?"

"Dirk? He's in his room. Won't come out."

"Why?"

"He's, like, really miserable. Depressed or something, I'm not sure. The whole thing seems to have hit him pretty hard. He's like Darth Vader on valium. Hasn't said a word since we got back, just stares glumly out the window."

"What? It's me who's gotten in trouble. Mom grounded me, and I've been suspended! Anyway, I won't be at school for a few days. Get him to call me. Or come and see me. He owes me that much at least! Also, I found Grousammer's diary—there's something in it I want to talk to him about."

"Okay, I'll get him to come and see you. But he's locked himself in his room right now. I'll try and talk to him later."

"Uh-oh, here comes Mom. Gotta go! See ya, Chris!"

"Later, Sooz!"
Click.

~~June~~ MiSeRY 3
All is lost. Though not on the field. But
who cares? Only the Sports Lord.

Whiteshields School Newsletter

Sports

Santa Ana Prep Utterly Annihilated

by Dwayne Smith

Santa Ana Prep was destroyed yesterday by Whiteshields.
In a blistering display of baseball skill, Santa Ana Prep—
favorites to win the division championships—were beaten
by six runs! After the game, Sal Malik, captain, said it
was due to the skill of his team, and the tactical know-
how of his cocaptain, Dirk Lloyd. Dirk was described by
Sal as a master tactician, and vital to the future success
of Whiteshields. Malik calls him his "Evil Genius."
Coach Hogan said, "At this rate we'll be through to

And as for this . . . Bah! The fools!

Whiteshields School Report: **DIRK LLOYD, 7th Gr.**
Teacher: **Mr. Havering**

BIOLOGY	Needs regular help to ensure progress at times	Making progress with some help overall	Making satisfactory progress overall	Making good progress	Achieves a consistently high standard overall
KNOWLEDGE OF SUBJECT STUDIED					✓
SCIENTIFIC METHODOLOGY					✓
RECORDING & PRESENTATION OF WORK				✓	

EFFORT	Needs to improve	Varies	Satisfactory	Good	Very good	Excellent
		✓				

Teacher's comment:

Dirk is a difficult pupil. His work is outstanding when it comes to predators, toxins, insects, bacteria (especially epidemics), and genetics. However, when I asked the class to cooperate on a biodiversity and green-issues project, Dirk protested that "plants are a breeding ground for elves and other vermin." He then drew up a list of "flaws and despicable weaknesses" in human DNA and turned in a report on how to genetically engineer and clone humans "for greater combat efficiency." Later, I found him standing behind me measuring the dimensions of my own skull and making notes for its modification.

Part Four:
Anguish and Joy

The BLACK HAND of DespAir

Dirk sat on the edge of the sofa, his head in his hands. Opposite him were Wings and Randle, the child psychologists. He'd been forced to put up with these weekly sessions ever since he had arrived on earth. Usually, Dirk was contemptuously dismissive of their therapies, their crackpot theories, and strange remedies based on that most bizarre of bizarre things—human psychology. As he kept telling them, he wasn't really human so none of this would work on him.

Or so he had believed. Now he wasn't so sure. Maybe they were right. Maybe he *was* suffering from Post-Traumatic Stress, and maybe he really *did* have a Dissociative Personality Disorder, or whatever they had called it. Perhaps he was just an overimaginative little kid who'd invented the whole Dark Lord thing to cover up some other horrible event or trauma.

His spell, the spell he'd created that he'd been convinced would open a portal between the planes hadn't worked. It didn't even seem like it could ever have worked. His Ring was just a ring. It probably never had any powers at all, and was just some ring bought from one of those fantasy role-playing websites or something, years ago. Maybe the Cloak really was just some kind of Harry Potter merchandising. The spell of the Sinister Hand was all in his mind as well. He'd probably just stolen a report card from some teacher's desk, and made up in his own mind all that stuff about sending off his left hand on its own, using soul power.

And because of his delusion, his *madness*, Sooz was going to be suspended and/or possibly expelled from school. Maybe even persecuted by "coppers." Or was it "prosecuted"? He could never remember.

Anyway, he'd gotten her into a lot of trouble. And she was his . . . He wanted to say follower or servitor, but realized that was probably delusional too. She was his friend. One of only two or three real friends he had in the whole world. But then again, maybe somewhere in the world he actually had some real parents. Once, that thought would have filled him with horror. Now he wasn't so sure. He began to tear up, as if he was about to cry. How could that be? Dark Lords don't cry!

Pulling himself together, he choked back his tears and looked up. His face was empty of feeling, pale and wan.

"Maybe you're right, Professor Randle," said Dirk.

"Umm, I'm Dr. Wings—that's Professor . . ."

Randle cut him off, "Let the boy speak, Wings, you idiot," he said, irritated.

Wings glared back at him. Dirk half-expected him to make a face, or stick his tongue out at Randle, but he didn't, though he looked like he really wanted to.

Dirk smiled weakly and went on. "But I can't remember anything of my life before I came to earth. Or before I created the delusion that I came to earth. I can't remember my parents, or any other life, except that of a Dark Lord, fallen to earth and trapped in the body of a human child. But the memories must be there, they must be—for all that Lord of Darkness stuff is just an illusion, isn't it?"

"This is excellent progress, my boy, excellent!" said Professor Randle.

"Quite so—the first step on the road to recovery is recognizing that you have a problem!" said Wings, as he reached into his pocket and popped a piece of gum into his mouth. He began to chew laboriously. He offered one to Dirk.

Dirk stared at the package for a moment. The last time Wings had offered one of those, Dirk had been convinced it was some kind of trick, an attempt to drug him. This time he took the entire packet from him. Wings looked rather alarmed for a moment, but

Dirk just took one and handed the package back. He chewed on the gum, savoring the minty flavor. Maybe he could create gum, if he ever made it back to his Inner Sanctum . . . but he caught himself. There was no Inner Sanctum, no Iron Tower of Despair, nestled in the lee of Mount Dread, no Gates of Doom. It was all in his mind.

"I've been having this recurring nightmare, as well," said Dirk. He explained about the White Beast that pursued him nearly every night, chasing him through his mind like one of those inescapable dooms he used to send against his enemies (well, so-called, of course).

Randle narrowed his eyes, and Wings frowned. Then Wings's face brightened as an idea came to him.

He spoke enthusiastically, "The White Beast is probably a subconscious manifestation of whatever trauma it is that has driven your mind into inventing this complex delusion. It is your mind trying to let it out, to express it. The trauma wants to come forth, to be recognized, but your conscious mind doesn't want to see it, wants to keep it buried. It is as if your unconscious mind is hunting your conscious mind!"

He turned to Randle and grinned triumphantly, as if to say, "I got there before you did, so stick that in your pipe and smoke it!"

Randle screwed his face up and turned away, looking irritated. Then he sighed and said grudgingly, "I suppose you may be right."

Dirk raised his eyes. These two were more inter-
ested in petty one-upmanship than actually helping
him. Better get them back on track, he thought, so he
said imperiously, as if commanding them to help him,
"How can I get my real life back?"

"Ah, well, psychotherapy is probably the answer,"
said Randle.

"Maybe even some hypnotherapy—see if we can
bring those memories of your real life back to the surface," said Wings.

"But we have to be careful with that," said Randle,
addressing Wings. "We mustn't bring the trauma to
the surface yet, just reestablish memories of his early
childhood. He isn't ready to deal with the trauma yet."

"Of course," said Wings testily. "What do you think
I am, an idiot?!"

Randle nodded slightly, and made a gesture with
his hands, as if to indicate that, yes, he did think Wings
was an idiot, as a matter of fact. But then Randle caught
himself, as he realized he'd overstepped the mark a bit,
especially as Wings narrowed his eyes and gave Randle
a murderous stare. Professor Randle looked sheepish
and then brightened up, as he'd just thought of something to say that would appease Wings.

"You're highly trained in hypnosis, Wings, aren't
you? One of the best! We could try a hypnotherapy session with Dirk right away, if he wants—and if his guardian, Mrs. Purejoie, gives permission," said Randle.

Wings did seem pacified by the flattery. "Indeed, that's true; I even teach hypnosis techniques. What do you think, Dirk. Shall we try it?" he said.

Dirk sighed. He knew all about hypnosis. Vampires used it to bewilder their prey. He'd used spells of hypnosis in the past to get information out of victims quickly, if there wasn't time for torture. It was a powerful tool, but it was only when he came to earth that he learned it could be done without magic at all, just with the power of suggestion. And that would never work on a Dark Lord—his will was simply too strong. Then he realized he was fantasizing again. He was just a kid, and they were adults—of course it would work.

"Okay," said Dirk. "I'll try. Anything that might help me get my memories back. I just want to be a normal kid and get on with my life."

"Very good, my boy, very good," said Wings. "You really are doing so very well!"

"Yes," said Randle. "I'm sure we'll have you cured in no time at all! Well, a few months at least—these things do actually take a bit of time, you know."

With that, they started to set things up. Randle went off to talk to Mrs. Purejoie, and returned a few minutes later with her written permission, which Dirk had to sign as well. Reflexively, he went for his Ring, meaning to use it to imprint his seal on the document, but then realized what he was doing, and simply signed it: "Dirk Lloyd."

Then they got Dirk to sit comfortably in Dr. Jack's large leather chair. Wings said he was going to use something called Progressive Relaxation Hypnotic Induction. He began to drone quietly to Dirk, telling him that he was falling asleep, that his eyelids were getting heavy, and so on—just like the stuff Dirk had seen on TV. But it didn't work. Dirk couldn't help saying things like: "No, they're not, my eyelids aren't heavy! They're only tiny pieces of human skin, how can they be heavy?" He was reverting to type. After a while, Wings stopped.

"Listen, Dirk," he said. "You've got to help me out here—it's almost impossible to hypnotize someone who doesn't want to be hypnotized. You have to relax. You have to *want* to go under. Trust us—we know what we're doing!"

Trust them? thought Dirk to himself. That was the problem. He wasn't a trusting kind of person—he always assumed people were self-serving, treacherous, and cunning, just like him . . . Except that he wasn't, of course. It was all in his mind. He was just another human child. What a ghastly thought! He sighed resignedly.

"Okay, Dr. Wings, I'll try," he said.

"Good boy," said Wings.

And this time Dirk did go under. Wings asked him to think back, to try and recall his first memories of his father. Dirk twitched, and wrung his hands together, as if he was struggling to remember.

But then suddenly he said, "I remember now, I remember! It was so long ago, many millennia in the past. The First Age they called it. The White Wizard— Gamulus the Good! He was my father! But he rejected me—he said I would never be a Holy Priest-Wizard. I was too selfish, too self-absorbed. He threw me out of the academy, and cursed me, banished me from his sight. He said I had the taint of evil, and that he'd made a mistake in thinking he could bring me up in the Light. I was a thing of Darkness, and all this because I had dabbled in the black arts! Ha, what did the old fool know anyway? I didn't need their fusty teachers, full of lectures about self-control, moderation, and love for all living things. I didn't need their White Words of Power and their Books of Blessed Spells. I would create my own, build my own Academy, an Academy of the Moon, an Academy of the Night, and outstrip them all. I would show them, show him, my puffed-up father—I'd show him how truly great I was, and then one day, they would come to me and beg for knowledge, beg for forgiveness! I am the Great Dirk! I would crush him, and his Academy of Holy Knowledge. I would . . ."

"Umm, yes, well. That's enough, Dirk, that's enough," said Wings.

Dirk fell silent, sinking back into his hypnotic sleep.

"Extraordinary," whispered Wings to Randle, "I've never seen this kind of entrenched delusion before, it's remarkable! So perfectly constructed."

Randle whispered back, "Sounds like maybe his father was some kind of fire-and-brimstone evangelist preacher or something. He's obviously got some serious issues with him. Why not ask him about his mother? Maybe that will dredge up something more normal."

"Good idea," said Wings, popping another piece of gum into his mouth. Randle's eyes flickered with irritation. Wings's constant gum chewing really got on his nerves.

"Now, Dirk, let us go back, right back. What can you remember about your mother? Who was she?" said Wings.

Dirk turned uncomfortably in the leather armchair. His face wrinkled up in distress.

"Mother . . . Mother," he said. Then he smiled. "She loved me. She used to feed me. Sweet milk and . . . blood," Dirk's voice seemed to trail off, and he began to shift about in the chair as if he didn't really want to talk about it.

Wings and Randle exchanged looks of fascinated surprise.

"This one could make our careers," Randle whispered. "We could write a book about him!"

WINGS AND RANDLE, PSYCHOS

"I know, I know," said Wings, shushing Randle into silence with his hands. "Go on, Dirk, tell us more about your mother."

Dirk spoke dreamily, "She was beautiful. Pale and dark, her eyes were as black as night, but her lips were bright, like rubies. She was old, very old but young, so young. A queen, in fact, her blood was royal. Well, her original blood that is—she tended to, errr . . . borrow blood from others. She did that a lot, in fact."

Wings and Randle seemed even more confused. Wings whispered, "Maybe she had leukemia or a kidney disease. Sounds like she had to have a lot of blood transfusions. Or dialysis, perhaps."

"And died young because of it, possibly? Maybe that's something he hasn't really come to terms with, do you think?" said Randle.

"Could be. Wait, he's about to say something," said Wings.

"She was Queen of the Nightwalkers, an ancient people who had their city at Sunless Keep. She told me one day that my father came there once, and that she'd ensorcelled him, tricked him into loving her—though I couldn't see why she needed to trick him. Who could not love that Dread Queen of the Night, the Dark Mistress of the Underworld, my mother, Oksana the Pale?"

Wings and Randle listened, fascinated by what

they were hearing, Wings chewing gum, and Randle stroking his chin like the caricature of the professor he was.

Dirk continued. "So it was that I was born out of the union of a White Wizard and a Vampire Queen . . ."

"Oh, this is hopeless," said Randle, throwing his hands up in despair. "It's still all vampires and wizards—he's making it all up again!"

"Wait a minute, he's going to say something else," said Wings.

"My father, Gamulus the Good, had fled Sunless Keep as soon as he'd had the chance, somehow breaking the bonds of the enchantment that held him. But when he learned that he'd fathered a son, he came for me. He came with Holy Fire and Blessed Steel, with Hawthorn Spears, hardened in the Sacred Flames of the Temple of Life, specifically made for the bursting of Vampire hearts. He came with an army of Paladins sworn to eradicate the Undead and all their works. They destroyed Sunless Keep, wrested me from the bosom of my loving mother, and slew her there in the Crypts. Then my father took me to the Academy of Holy Knowledge, to bring me up as one of their own."

Dirk fell into silence. Tears ran from his eyes.

Randle whispered, "That's it! It's all made up nonsense, but that's why. I bet you his father murdered his mother in real life!"

"Yes, it all makes sense," said Wings.

Randle continued with the idea. "And then Dirk ran away from home, constructing this elaborate fantasy to soften the horror of it all."

"It could even be that his father is in prison right now," said Wings excitedly.

"We should check the records," said Randle.

"Yes. It's fascinating, fascinating. Did you record it all?"

"Oh yes, got it all on tape. I suppose we should wake him now, he's looking upset," said Randle.

"Yes, don't want to make him suffer anymore! We have to take it gently, step by step," said Wings.

"Wake up, Dirk!" he said loudly. He clicked his fingers.

Dirk woke with a start. He looked around, confused. "Did you find anything out? Professor Wandle? Dr. Rings?" asked Dirk.

"That's Professor *Randle*," said Randle tersely.

"Oh, let the boy speak," snapped Wings, more than happy to pop one back at Randle.

Randle raised his eyes heavenward and ignored him. He said to Dirk, "Yes, we did, Dirk; it was very, very interesting."

"So who were my parents?" said Dirk eagerly.

"It's best we don't talk about that yet," said Wings as he pulled the pack of gum out of his pocket.

Randle gave Wings a look of pure irritation, snatched the gum out of his hand, and thrust it into his own pocket. Wings looked at him, quite astonished. Then Randle said, "Trust us, Dirk, it wasn't really clear who they were. We must try a few more treatments, so we can get to the bottom of this."

Wings stepped over next to Randle, as if he was maneuvering himself into a position where he could make a grab for the gum, and said to Dirk, "There are a few other angles we'd like to pursue as well, but we'll let you know about them as soon as we can!"

Randle shoved Wings away with his elbow and said, "Oh yes, indeed. We'll say good-bye for now, dear boy. You are really doing very well indeed, very well! We have to work on our strategy for your next course of treatment."

They left the room. Dirk sat by the window, exhausted. He could hear Wings and Randle talking to Mrs. Purejoie in the hall for a few minutes. Once Dirk would have tried to eavesdrop on their conversation, but now he just couldn't be bothered. Then he heard the front door opening and shutting. He watched Wings and Randle walk to their car. It looked like Wings was berating Randle quite angrily. Randle suddenly stopped, pulled the pack of gum from his pocket, and scattered the pieces all over the road. With that, he threw the empty pack into Wings's face and stomped off to the car. Wings stood there incredulously for a moment and then made a face at Randle's back. He picked a piece of gum off the ground. Randle was just opening the car door when Wings angrily hurled it at him. It struck him squarely on the back of the head, bounced off, and skittered into the bushes. Randle froze in shock for a moment, unsure as to how to respond. After a second or two, he just cleared his throat as if nothing had happened and got into the car. Wings grinned triumphantly. Then he bent down, picked up another piece of the gum, popped it into his mouth, and chewed ostentatiously before following Randle into the car.

Dirk shook his head despairingly. What a pair. And to think he was putting all his hopes and fears in their hands.

That evening, Chris came to see him. Dirk was slumped in his chair, listlessly gazing out the window.

"What's going on, Your Dirkness?" he asked.

"Don't call me that. I'm no longer the Dark Lord. I am just Dirk," said Dirk miserably.

"What do you mean? What are you saying?" said Chris, shocked at what he heard.

"I am nothing. Just a boy. It was all a delusion, a kind of madness. A Dissociative Personality Disorder, as the psychologists called it," said Dirk.

Chris couldn't believe what he was hearing. "But

they're idiots, those two. Wings and Randle. You said so! And what about 'Them'?"

Dirk looked at him inquisitively.

"You know, 'Them.' 'They.' The do-gooders, the teachers, parents, social services and the rest, out there trying to control you, trying to control us! Aren't we rebels anymore?" said Chris.

"No, we're not, we're just kids," said Dirk glumly. "It's over. It was all a dream. A game. A stupid delusion."

Chris scowled. This was awful! He didn't want to hear *this*. Without the Dark Lord, the Lloyd of Dirkness, they were all just kids again, powerless kids with no control over their lives. Hopeless teenagers. Just another bunch of school kids trying to make it to adulthood without too much damage. And without the Dark Lord, how were they going to save Sooz?

Dirk went on. "That fire proved it. It's a good thing. It burned out the madness in my head. What a delusion! As if I could travel to another plane—it's ridiculous!"

Chris sat on the bed, shoulders slumped in despair. It hadn't really mattered to him, or the rest of the Dark Lord's Court in Exile, whether it was really true or not. What really mattered was that Dirk believed it was true. He made it *feel* real. His belief made it worth playing along with. Without that the whole thing became meaningless, just another game.

Chris still couldn't quite believe Dirk was serious.

"But what about Hasdruban the Pure—don't you still want revenge?" he asked.

"Ha! What of him? I am defeated. Utterly defeated. Hasdruban has won. Though, of course, there never was a Hasdruban in the first place!" retorted Dirk.

They sat in despairing silence for a while. Then Dirk said, "How is Sooz, by the way?"

"Not good," said Chris. "In fact, I wanted to talk to you about that. She's taken the rap, you know, so you're off the hook. Grousammer's threatened to hand her over to the police. He could be bluffing, but if he does she might be charged or something, which will give her a criminal record. And she's been suspended from school."

Dirk was appalled. "I had no idea . . . ," he said. "By the Nine Netherworlds, what have I done?" He put his head in his hands and rocked back and forth.

Chris went on. "She could be expelled. Maybe even sent away to one of those special schools, or something. We might not see her ever again." Chris's voice cracked and he turned away.

Dirk looked up, shocked. "Never see her again . . . ?"

"It's possible," said Chris. "It's up to Grousammer, really. Depends how far he wants to go with it."

Dirk thought for a moment and said, "I don't really care what happens to me anymore. I could go and say I burned down the pavilion. Get her off the hook. What do you think?"

"I don't know, Dirk. Maybe. But that would make them suspicious. They'd want to know why she said she did it. It could just end up with both of you getting in trouble, and what's the point of that? She wouldn't want that either. Actually, when I spoke to her, she was more upset about the fact that you hadn't gone to see her, or even called her."

Dirk looked away guiltily. "I don't think I can look her in the face at the moment, I feel so terrible."

"Well, you should go and see her. You owe her that much, at least!" said Chris.

"Anyway, why *did* she 'take the rap' as you humans say? Or we humans, I mean," asked Dirk.

"Don't you know?" said Christopher angrily. He couldn't keep the jealousy out of his voice as he said, "I think she's got a thing for you. God knows why!" Then he got ahold of himself and went on. "Also, actually, she thought you'd pull something out of the bag to rescue her, to get her off the hook. We all thought that—the Lloyd of Dirkness, he'll save her. Cast a spell or pull off some trick or scam or whip up a campaign to free her. The Child of the Night is innocent! Free her now! That kind of thing."

Dirk looked away in embarrassment. "There is nothing I can do. I am powerless. I'm just a kid, for goodness' sake!"

"Don't you mean for evil's sake?" said Chris

attempting to raise a smile, to try and get back something of the old Dirk.

"No, I mean for goodness' sake," said Dirk emphatically. "Look, I'll think about turning myself in to save her, but that's about all I can do. But, as you say, what's the point if that just means we'll both go down? In fact, what's the point of anything? Might as well just give up . . ." He turned to stare out the window, making it obvious that he wanted to be alone.

Chris sighed. He couldn't think of anything else to say anyway, so he left, leaving Dirk to his despair.

As he left, he heard Dirk muttering under his breath, "Maybe the White Beast will find me and end it all . . . Or is that too just a dream?" Chris frowned. Dirk didn't sound good. And it was really annoying Chris. His parents could see something was wrong with Dirk and they were all over him—and ignoring Chris completely. Should he start moping around and staring into space all day? Would they pay more attention to him then?

And Dirk wasn't treating Sooz right either—first he asked Chris to steal from her, and now he was leaving her in the lurch. In fact, the more Chris thought about it, the more he thought about how the only reason he put up with Dirk (well, actually *liked* Dirk, in fact, but right now he wasn't prepared to admit that) was because he was fun to be around and made him laugh. Right now Dirk wasn't much fun to be around.

Akram Malik, Sal's father, reversed his car into
the parking spot, listening to a ball game on the
radio. He didn't wonder why the only spaces that
were empty in the entire parking lot were this one
and the two spaces on either side of it, almost as
if people were deliberately avoiding this area. Nor
did he notice the cardboard sign someone had
hastily propped up against the edge of the
pavement. They'd scrawled on it the words
BEWARE THE CURSED PARKING SPOT OF DOOM! He was
too wrapped up in the game.

He noticed a blind man with a guide dog
walking past the front of his car. He felt an
inexplicable urge to slam his foot down on the
accelerator and run the poor man down. He
tittered at the thought. He couldn't understand
it—his own father had been blind, and Akram was
a volunteer at the local charity for the blind. Why
would he want to run one of them over? Hurriedly
he turned the ignition off, and got out of the car.
The feeling of evil malice that seemed to have
come over him faded after a few minutes, and he
began to feel a lot better.

But on his return, he found the back bumper
of his car had fallen off. On closer inspection, he
could see that most of it had literally rusted away.
In half an hour.

Akram frowned. Nearby, an old woman, gray-haired, stooped, and shriveled, sat on a bench, feeding the birds bread crumbs.

"It's cursed! That parking spot. Cursed I tell you!" she screeched.

BREAKFAST AT PUREJOIES

The next day was a school holiday and Dirk was woken in the usual way.

"Good morning, Dirk. Get up, sweetheart!" said Mrs. Purejoie, as she did every morning, drawing the curtains and flooding the room with light.

"Mornings are never good, and don't call me . . . ," Dirk began, in the usual way, but then he sighed, remembering. Today was his first day as a human child, a normal kid. It was going to be difficult to adjust. To get back to normal. He gave up on his usual greetings and simply said, "Good morning, Mrs. Purejoie . . ."

"Call me Hilary," she said, as she did every morning.

"Good morning, Hilary," said Dirk without thinking.

At this, Mrs. Purejoie rushed over and gave him a big hug. Dirk cringed under this onslaught of love like a kid who wanted to be feared as a terrible Dark Lord rather than hugged by a kind and loving mother. For a moment, Dirk thought she would crush all the life out of him but soon she relented and said, "Does this mean you don't want to be Darth Vader anymore, Dirk, dear?"

Dirk made a face. He didn't really want to talk about it, but he said in a barely audible mumble, "Not Darth Vader, you fool, more like the Emperor Palpatine . . ." Then he trailed off—what was the point? So he said more loudly, "Sort of, Mrs. . . . er, Hilary."

"That's just wonderful, dear, just wonderful!" She gave him another suffocating hug. Dirk groaned inwardly. He wasn't sure if he could manage trying to be normal. It seemed so . . . odd. She leaned back a bit, and looked at him. She smiled.

"Well done, Dirk, well done," she said. "It'll take time, but you're going to get better and better, really you are. Dr. Wings and Professor Randle said this would be a sign of healing, of getting better! How right they were."

Dirk smiled insincerely at her, and then looked out the window. All this patting on the back, the hugging and stuff, it made him feel rather uncomfortable. As for Wings and Randle—how did those two idiots ever qualify for *anything*, let alone make it to doctor and professor?

Mrs. Purejoie returned to the attack and hugged him again, saying, "You're such a sweet little boy, Dirk, I could eat you up! You're such a . . . cutie pie!" With that, she gave him a tickle in the ribs.

That was too much for Dirk. "Oh, please!" he said. "Give it a rest. I may be delusional, but I'm still a boy! Enough already!" Dirk groaned inside. If only he really was a Dark Lord. He wouldn't have to put up with this for long!

Mrs. Purejoie backed off. She knew what boys were like. Too much love could embarrass them. In fact, it was much the same with grown men, who often pretended not to like being called cutie pies too.

"Well, what would you like for breakfast, my darling?" said Mrs. Purejoie, changing the subject.

"Whatever . . . ," muttered Dirk ungraciously.

Instead of snapping at him for being rude, Mrs. Purejoie smiled even more. After all, from her point of view this was the typical response of your average teenage boy, so it was good to hear. Normally, she might have gotten something like "I demand the roasted hearts of my vanquished foe!" or "Souls! I will drink Souls for breakfast," so it was nice to have something normal for once, even if it was a little curt.

"Well, have a shower, brush your teeth, and get dressed. I'll make you some eggs. Your favorite!"

With that she gave him a kiss on the forehead, which Dirk endured with a grimace, and then left the room.

Eggs his favorite? He *had* said that once, Dirk thought to himself, but he'd meant the Egg of Life of course, that first egg out of which the universe itself was born. Eating of its shell would give you power beyond the comprehension of mortal and immortal alike! He'd never found the Egg of Life, but if he ever did . . . But that was all in his mind. There was no Egg of Life. Only fried eggs on toast, a la Purejoie. Dirk brightened at that. Actually, fried eggs on toast with some bacon . . . yum! He got out of bed, threw off his Grim Reaper pajamas (he'd had to get those custom made—you couldn't just buy them, and it'd taken a lot of persuasion to get permission) and got into the shower.

A short while later, he was sitting at the breakfast table opposite Christopher. In front of him was a plate of fried eggs on toast with bacon on the side. The smell of it made his mouth water. But he couldn't eat it yet. He had to wait for Mrs. Purejoie. They always had to wait for Mrs. Purejoie, so she could say grace. Dirk began to drum his fingers on the table, as he did every time they ate. Chris raised his eyes heavenward. He knew Dirk hated the blessing and the waiting but the same old finger drumming was getting a bit tedious these days. At last, Mrs. Purejoie came in. Dirk rubbed his hands together with impatient anticipation.

"Come along, Mrs. . . . er, Hilary, let's get going, shall we?" said Dirk briskly as if he was in charge, and she was some kind of servant.

Mrs. Purejoie smiled at Dirk indulgently. She sat down and said, "Holy Father bless this food. For what

MY pAjAMAS

we are about to receive, may the Lord make us truly thankful." With that she made the sign of the cross and indicated that they could all start.

The first time this had happened, all those months ago, Dirk had freaked out. After all, if a Dark Lord were to eat food that was blessed it would burn his mouth like bright sunlight on the pale, vulnerable skin of the Vampire. Blessed food was holy food. A Dark Lord couldn't eat that! But he was used to it now. In any case, he wasn't really a Dark Lord so it didn't matter. He dug in, crushing the egg yolks as if they were the eyes of Hasdruban the Pure and mashing them up with the toast and bacon, until it was a goopy mass. He always imagined eggs on toast were a kind of Blood Porridge, made from the eyes of the White Wizard, toasted Halfling-flesh, and the blood of a Brown Elf.

He began shoveling it into his mouth. He talked through the munching, saying, "How sweet are the eyes of the Wizard!" and "Hmm, crunchy Halfling." He always made comments like this at breakfast, which usually set Christopher off giggling. But today Christopher didn't seem in the mood.

Dirk looked over at Mrs. Purejoie. She was doing what she usually did—ignoring him. She'd long ago given up trying to change this behavior at the table, and she'd become pretty accomplished at just tuning him out when it was time to eat. That used to make

Dirk feel like he'd "won," that he'd put something over on the Pure Guardians, but today it didn't seem right. The running commentary he usually kept up while eating began to trail off.

Mrs. Purejoie looked over at him. "Good boy," she said, as if he were a dog. Dirk raised his eyes. He wasn't a dog, and he didn't want to be a boy. He didn't even want to be good. But he *was* a boy. And maybe it was time to think about being "good." He needed to fit in, to be normal, just like any other boy. So he just smiled, and thanked Mrs. Purejoie for the excellent eggs on toast.

After breakfast, Mrs. Purejoie left to preach a sermon at her church. Dr. Jack had suggested a day trip somewhere, but neither Christopher nor Dirk were in the mood. In any case, it was a gray, drizzly day, not the best for a trip. Dr. Jack made some suggestions, but Dirk and Chris said they wanted to play a computer game, much to Jack's annoyance. He tried to persuade them otherwise, but in the end he gave up and took himself off to the living room with a book leaving Chris and Dirk to their own devices.

They went upstairs to Chris's computer, but when it came down to it neither of them could be bothered. The whole pavilion/Sooz/fire thing was really getting them down. They just sat on the bed in Chris's room, not saying a word.

Eventually Chris spoke. "I've got to talk to you about something."

Dirk waved a hand imperiously. "Speak."

"You have to talk to Sooz," said Christopher.

Dirk looked sick at the prospect. "But what do I say? 'Sorry'? What difference is that going to make?" he said despondently.

"You've got to talk to her—she's taking the blame. And she's your friend. She deserves better," insisted Christopher.

Dirk looked miserable. He'd fought endless wars, commanded vast armies of fearsome monsters, burned cities, built Black Towers of Doom, battled mighty Paladins in hand-to-hand combat, cast terrible spells that darkened the skies, and so much more, but talking to a teenage Goth girl seemed to terrify the life out of him. And she was one of his minions—he shouldn't be scared of her. But none of that Evil Overlord stuff was real of course. It was all in his mind. And she was a friend, not a minion. Dirk sighed. Maybe this is what it meant to feel "guilt." Christopher was right; he had to talk to her.

"Okay—I'll call her or something," he said unconvincingly.

"No, man, that's not good enough. You have to go and see her, talk to her face-to-face. After all, it ought to be you taking the blame, not her!" shouted

Christopher angrily. Dirk was beginning to annoy him again. He wasn't treating Sooz right.

Dirk tutted in irritation, but he had to admit Christopher had a point. "Oh, all right, I'll go over and see her."

That surprised Chris. He'd regretted immediately losing his temper and raising his voice—that was guaranteed not to work with Dirk as it was virtually impossible to persuade Dirk to do something he didn't want to do. In fact, it was incredible that he was even considering what Christopher had to say. Nor had he gone into a Dark Lord rant about how nobody should tell him what to do.

Christopher pushed a bit more. "You might as well go this morning. Nothing else to do today. And there's one more thing—Sooz told me to tell you that she found something in Grousammer's office. Something he'd written in his diary. She wants to talk to you about it."

Dirk shrugged. "Okay," he said. With that, he got up and left.

Christopher could hardly believe it. That had been a lot easier than he'd expected. But he knew it was for the best. One of the worst things about the whole situation for Sooz was that Dirk hadn't even been in touch with her. He owed her that at least.

Dirk went into his room and put on his jacket. Then he had a thought. He opened the wardrobe to look for his Cloak of Endless Night. It had been carefully hung up by Mrs. Purejoie. It smelled clean and fresh. She'd washed it using one of those sickeningly fragrant fabric softeners called Summer Breeze or Spring Delight or some other absurdly trite name. Why couldn't she bathe it in blood or something? Not only that—Dirk realized that it'd been *ironed*. Probably by Dr. Jack, who had to do the ironing in the Purejoie household.

Dirk scowled. Dark Lords didn't wear ironed cloaks that smelled of fabric softener, for evil's sake! How could they do this to him? Also, he wondered whether being washed and ironed would affect the power of the magic Blood Glyphs. Could they have been damaged in some way? But then he caught himself. It wasn't a real Cloak of Endless Night, and the Purejoies were only doing what a million parents did every day, all over the world. He bundled the Cloak under his arm, and set off for Sooz's.

He decided to take a detour past the school. It hadn't been long since the fire, and he wanted to check out the garden. He wanted to get rid of his Cloak, and the garden might be the best place to do that. The Cloak just reminded him of his past madness, his sickness. No, it was time to dispose of it once and for all, along with the whole Dark Lord delusion. He'd also take a look at the pavilion. Revisit the scene of the crime as it were.

The CLOAK

The pavilion had been completely burned down. Nothing much remained. He could see a couple of figures picking their way through the blackened wreckage. Fire investigators, no doubt, trying to establish the cause of the fire. That got Dirk thinking. Surely they would find Sooz's gas cooker? And people didn't deliberately start fires using a gas cooker. Maybe that was something worth mentioning to Sooz. Might work in her favor. He owed her that much at least! It was also very odd, the way the pavilion had gone up so quickly. Humans were obsessed with health and safety—didn't they normally fireproof structures like this?

Dirk sighed and turned away. Well, it was all in the hands of the "adults" now. They'd decide what was what.

He walked toward the garden. Up ahead, he spotted what he'd been looking for. Another fire. A small fire though—a bonfire of weeds and branches from some recently cleared garden. He glanced around. Nobody was nearby so he walked over and threw his Cloak on the flames. It was time to burn away all the nonsense, all that Dark Lord madness. Cleanse his mind with fire! The black Cloak began to sputter, and then burst into flames, crackling angrily. The red Blood Glyphs of Power began to glow brightly. Dirk reached for his Ring. That could go on the flames as well. But then he gaped in astonishment . . .

The Cloak had burned away almost in an instant. But not the Glyphs. They rose slowly up from the fire, and began to spin in the air, revolving around and around like a firecracker, faster and faster with a hissing whir. Dirk could hardly believe his eyes! And then the Glyphs smoldered like phosphorous, as if they were burning their way through the very fabric of space and time itself. They were melting the air, leaving a strange blackness behind.

Abruptly the Glyphs disappeared, revealing some kind of window, just hanging there in space. Dirk could make out shapes—hills, mountains, and a red-tinged sky. He recognized what he saw.

He was looking into another world. That realm he called his own. The Darklands . . .

Dirk stood there, dumbfounded. This meant . . . this meant it was all real! He really was the Dark Lord of the Darklands! How could he have been so stupid? Of course he was! Oh, that Hasdruban—he was cunning, oh so cunning. He'd nearly had him fooled, nearly had him believing it all, nearly had him convincing himself he was nothing but a puny human child. A deluded child.

Oh, but he had to admire the brilliance of it. It was inspired, a scheme so ingenious it was worthy of himself. But now he'd uncovered the truth! The despair and the sadness fell away, and a kind of black joy filled him, a wild exultation, a dark blossoming of resolve and determination. He *was* the Dark Lord, now more than ever!

Dirk rushed forward and tried putting his hand through the portal—maybe he didn't need any complicated rituals, maybe all he needed was to burn the Cloak to open a way. But his hand came up hard against what felt like thick, solid glass. It was only a window, a spyglass into the Darklands. Things were never that easy, after all. Dirk stepped back to observe. He was looking at a great rolling expanse of blasted heath that seemed to stretch away forever. Gray clouds hung over a mournful, dirty-water colored plain, studded with rocky outcrops and low hills. He recognized the Plains of Desolation.

Dirk noticed something near his field of view. Was that a figure, crouching in a muddy hollow, as if hiding? Dirk tried to concentrate, to make out the details. Suddenly the window moved, responding to his thoughts, and closed in on the figure. Dirk smiled. This was like old times. The magic obeyed his will, as all things should. Then he gasped. It was Gargon! His lieutenant, Dread

Gargon, the Hewer of Limbs, Captain of the Legions of Dread! And it was really him—not just some human dressed up, like that Morti character. He could see his skeletal body, the mighty talons and the bony ridges of his batlike wings.

"Gargon!" he shouted, but then he caught himself and looked around guiltily. He didn't want to draw any unwanted attention to himself, especially from the High Council of the White Shields or something. Besides, it was obvious that sound couldn't pass through the window.

He focused in. Gargon was cowering in fear, looking up at the sky furtively. Dirk tracked the window upward with his mind into the red-tinged sky of the Darklands. Aha! Eagle Riders, curse them. They made for a formidable foe—a human warrior riding on the back of a giant eagle, brought up together as nest mates, forever sworn to serve the White Wizard and the Commonwealth of Good Folk, may the Nether Gods eat their souls! They were flying high, and soon they had passed over.

Gargon sank to the ground, sobbing in relief. He was in a sorry state, beaten and bruised. It looked like he'd been on the run—perhaps for months. Poor Gargon! He'd probably been hunted all this time by those implacable fanatics, the Paladins of Righteousness. They would never rest until they'd hunted down all his followers. Well, there was nothing he could do about

WINDOW INTO THE DARKLANDS

it—yet. Gargon would have to survive as best he could until Dirk could get back.

Then Dirk noticed a great peak on the horizon: Mount Dread. In its foothills lay his Iron Tower. With that thought, the view shifted, flying across the blasted Plains of Desolation toward Mount Dread.

As the interplanar vision hurtled across the Plains, it passed over a troop of Orcs. Dirk could see they were in a bad way, panting with exhaustion, dirty and muddy—well, Orcs were always dirty and muddy, of course, but these also had tattered armor, and filthy, bloodstained makeshift bandages on various fresh wounds. They'd long ago thrown away their shields and weapons—these Orcs were on the run.

Judging from what remained of their military insignia, they were from the Legion of Merciless Mayhem, one of his elite Legions, made up of the most disciplined, hard-bitten veteran Orcs he could breed. They had been commanded by the Black Slayer, another one of his lieutenants. Once. Now they were a ragtag bunch of desperate runaways, fleeing for their lives.

Dirk couldn't understand it. What were they running from? After he'd been cast down to earth by Hasdruban, his armies would have dispersed, leaderless, been easy to defeat by those Commonwealth fanatics. Surely the war had been over for months? What was going on?

Then he saw their pursuers—Paladins! On large,

armored white chargers with bright white shields, their armor gleaming, and their pennoned lances at the ready. Fanatics, the lot of them. But they weren't pursuing hard—it was almost as if they were herding the Orcs somewhere. Dirk moved his view in the direction the Orcs were heading and zoomed in. A small wood. And there, a troop of white-coated Elvish archers, waiting in the trees! They bore gold sigils on the front of their coats, the symbol of the White Wizard. The white coats mirrored their pale skin, and the Wizard's symbol mirrored their golden hair. Sickeningly sartorial as always, thought Dirk. These were Templar Elves, an elite group who left their Elvish homelands to take up service with the White Wizard, sworn to serve him and protect the Temple of Life until death. More fanatics, just like the Paladins. And his Orcs were heading straight for them!

Dirk wanted to warn them somehow but there was nothing he could do. Suddenly the Templar Elves stepped as one into the open and unleashed a deadly volley of arrows. Half of the Orcs fell dead in their tracks. The rest just stopped, exhausted, all the fight knocked out of them. They just dropped to their knees and put their hands up over their heads, in the classic posture of Orcish submission and surrender. But the Paladins closed in and charged. They speared to death every last Orc . . . Dirk was shocked. Even he, a Dark

Lord, would accept surrender. Sure, he might have one in ten killed as a lesson to the others. All right, two in ten. But there was no point in just massacring everyone. There'd be no one left to pay taxes, no one left to dominate and control. No one to enslave and boss around. What was the point of that?

Was that what was happening? Was that the reason Gargon and the Orcs were on the run long after the war was over? The Commonwealth was trying to wipe out every last one of his troops? Dirk was horrified. These were his people, he'd bred them, trained them. They were his creations, his followers, his, his . . . his toys, blast it! How could Hasdruban take them away from him? It would take decades to replace them.

Hasdruban had to be stopped. Dirk had to get back to the Darklands. He had to save as much of his stuff as he could.

Then Dirk noticed that the window into another world was beginning to sputter—just like interference on TV, as if the signal was weakening. Quickly he moved the vision on—he wanted to take one last look at his Iron Tower of Despair before the window closed.

He forced the view up and across the Plains of Desolation, flying toward his Iron Tower at breakneck speed. And then he saw it silhouetted against the backdrop of Mount Dread. It looked pleasingly foreboding, a harbinger of doom. As the view neared, he noticed something wasn't quite right. Of course, he'd expected some damage—a few battlements torn down, the Chamber of Summoning at the top demolished at the least, but it wasn't that. Something else . . . Then he saw. It was pink! Bright pink!

"Noooo! They've painted it pink! Pink! How could they?" he wailed.

And around the spiked buttresses and iron-clad walls, now painted pink with purple flowers all over them, little winged fairy folk fluttered and gamboled in the air. Down below, people milled around the tower, laughing and drinking, having picnics, and listening to musicians and poets. They'd turned his Iron Tower of Despair into some kind of amusement park!

Dirk's face flushed with humiliation. How embarrassing. How dreadfully embarrassing. He could hardly bear to watch. The great Dark Lord's Tower, reduced to a pink-coated day-trip attraction!

Ah, that Hasdruban. Once again, Dirk had to admit it was a stroke of genius. What better way to mock and discredit the memory of a Dark Lord than by reducing his great works—that were meant to create fear and dread in the minds of those who looked upon them—to meaningless pink fluffiness? It was a propaganda masterstroke. And if Hasdruban succeeded in wiping out the rest of his followers there would be nothing left of the Dark Lord's legacy at all. With Dirk forever exiled on another plane, people would soon forget completely the original purpose of the Iron Tower of Despair, and its dread occupant. It would become Pink Fairy Towers or something ghastly like that—a family outing, a day trip for kids and fairies.

"Noooo!" wailed Dirk once more. Hasdruban would pay. By the Nine Netherworlds, he'd pay for this! This was worse than killing his troops. This was . . . desecration. Pink, for evil's sake! Dirk hesitated for a moment. Well, okay, it probably wasn't as bad as killing his Orcs and Goblins. Well, certainly from their point of view. But still, it was very, very annoying.

Furious revenge fantasies began to run through his mind like a storm-swollen river. Suddenly the window snapped shut. Just like that. At the last moment, something popped out, and landed on the ground with a glassy tinkling sound. Dirk reached down and picked up the object, his eyes narrowing.

Now he knew who he was! Now he would redouble his efforts—he would return to the Darklands. But first he had to rescue Sooz, get his people together here, sort things out on earth. *Then* he would work out how to get back. He examined the object in his hand. It was what he suspected—an Interplanar Soul Bottle. Certain magical creatures and races used these bottles to travel between the planes of existence, rather like the way humans put messages into bottles and cast them into the sea. Someone wanted to speak with him.

Carefully, he broke the magical seal on the bottle

and flipped its lid. There was a rush of smoke as something burst forth and formed into a thin, spindly humanoid shape before his eyes. Once the smoke cleared, Dirk found himself staring at a strange creature—humanlike, but with arms and legs that were very long and thin, with a shock of spiky salt-and-pepper hair. Its face was scrunched and compact, with sharp, spiky features. A tiny golden cap rested on its head. Dirk recognized the little being and his Royal Cap immediately—it was Foletto the Skirrit King. The Skirrits were a race of tiny Goblin-like beings who lived in between the worlds, in the interplanar spaces that run between the dimensions. They could be summoned—by both White and Black Wizards—and, for the right payment, be contracted to carry out various tasks and quests. Foletto, who was slightly shorter than Dirk, looked up at him, a puzzled expression on his scrunched-up face.

"I am looking for His Imperial Majesty, the Dark Lord of the Iron Tower . . . er," said the Skirrit King in a high voice. "You don't look like him, but you . . . Well, you *feel* like him."

Dirk nodded. "Greetings, Foletto. It is I, but I have been cursed and forced to inhabit the wretched body of a puny human child."

Comprehension dawned on the Skirrit's face. "Ah!" he exclaimed. "Hasdruban, I presume?" he said.

"Yes, it was Hasdruban. He has the upper hand at the moment, but soon I shall crush him utterly!" said Dirk.

Foletto raised a white, spiky eyebrow and looked Dirk up and down.

"Your situation doesn't look promising, I have to say," Foletto said. "And the body of a human boy—yuk! How disgusting! Still, I have come because I sensed you were trapped on this plane. Then you opened that convenient portal, no doubt to allow me through to this plane. Anyway, I thought you might need my help."

Dirk raised an eyebrow of his own. "Help? You mean you sensed an opportunity for profit, more likely," said Dirk.

"Ah, well, yes, now that you put it like that. My help does come at a price, of course. After all, we've had several mutually beneficial contracts in the past, so why not again? Except . . . Well, I don't know how to say this, so I'll just say it outright. Seeing your current state, I am not so sure you'll be able to pay," said Foletto.

Dirk's eyes narrowed. Foletto turning up out of the blue was a bit of rare good luck. And by the Nine Netherworlds, he could really use some help, stuck here on earth. Mentally he patted himself on the back for not ripping off the Skirrit King in the past and actually sticking to their previous deals. If he hadn't, Foletto wouldn't even be here.

He seemed to be under the impression that Dirk had

intended to summon him. But truth be told, Dirk had completely forgotten about the Skirrits and their King and in any case had no way of casting the summoning spell. Still, no sense letting Foletto know that! And anyway, why shouldn't he come whether or not Dirk called him? The power and essence of a Dark Lord always attracted creatures like this. They were drawn to him like a moth to a flame.

Dirk considered things for a moment. Then he said, "There is a task I would have you do. As to payment, what if I were to promise to give you whatever your heart desires if you come to me when I am once again ruling from my Iron Tower of Despair, and my powers have been regained?"

The Skirrit King gasped out loud, "Whatever my heart . . ." Foletto was obviously surprised. Things must be really bad for the Dark One for him to make such an offer. Carefully (you had to be especially careful when negotiating with the Sorcerer Supreme, even if he was in a tight spot), Foletto replied, "Umm, yes, despite your currently reduced state, I'm sure we can come to some agreement, Your Imperial Darkness."

And so the conversation went on . . .

WRATH OF THE GOTHS

Dirk arrived at Sooz's house, a thousand schemes and plots running through his head. He knocked on the door. After a short wait, the door opened and Sooz poked her head around the corner, a look of trepidation on her face. She probably thought he was the police or something, sent by Grousammer to arrest her. But at the sight of Dirk, she scowled angrily.

"Oh, it's you," she said sullenly. "Where've you been?"

"Greetings, Child of the Night!" Dirk said with a big grin on his face. He said this with such absurd glee and confidence, that Sooz's mouth, set in an angry line, twitched a bit at the corners.

"I shall use all my evil genius to see you liberated from the baleful influence of that tyrant Grousammer and you will be free to prowl the night like the sweet little Vampire you are," Dirk enthused.

This was too much for Sooz and she had to smile.

She shook her head ruefully, then laughed and said, "Dirk, it's good to see your crazy face!" With that she stepped forward and gave him a big hug.

Dirk froze. He just couldn't get used to this human hugging business. But after a moment or two he relented and put his arms around Sooz and hugged her back. Dirk had never really hugged another being before. Not in a thousand years. Sure, maybe he'd hugged a few to death, but that was different. This actually felt nice. He felt something odd . . . What was it? Ah yes, *affection*. He felt affection for Sooz. He wanted to protect her, to look after her.

At this thought, Dirk broke the embrace and coughed, embarrassed by his feelings.

Look after her like she was a pet, of course, he thought to himself desperately. Or a particularly good minion, an excellent lackey. That was it. Useful. Dark Lords didn't *like* people for themselves, didn't care for them out of affection and love, for goodness' sake. For *evil's* sake, I mean!

"You all right?" said Sooz.

Dirk didn't know what to make of these unexpected emotions. They had thrown him off balance. But he pulled himself together.

"Sooz," he said imperiously, "I beg your forgiveness for not coming to your aid more quickly, but I . . . was distracted."

"Distracted by what?" she said, scowling. "I really needed you!"

"I . . . Well, I . . ." Dirk couldn't bear to admit he'd lost his self-confidence, and given in to despair. A Dark Lord never admitted to weakness. Especially in front of a girl.

"I've been working on a . . . a plan . . . ," he added lamely.

"That's not what Chris said. He said you'd been depressed, like you'd given up or something."

Dirk screwed his face up in annoyance. That blabber-mouth Christopher! Then he sighed. Maybe sometimes you had to admit things, tell the truth even, especially to your friends. Or most loyal lackeys, rather.

He looked around shiftily, desperately trying to think of some other course of action. He could just deny it, as he would have done in the old days. But no, perhaps those times were gone for good. So he said, "I did get a little down, yes. And I'm sorry for it. I couldn't see a way out."

Sooz seemed to accept this. She said, "Well, we all feel like that sometimes. I certainly have, the last few days."

It suddenly dawned on Dirk just how bad a time Sooz must have been having. It can't have been anything like a Dark Lord losing his self-confidence, of course, but for her, in her world, it must have been quite frightening. Dirk couldn't believe it—he was beginning to experience another emotion. What was it called? Ah yes, *empathy*. Empathy and affection! All in the same day. Extraordinary.

"Anyway," Dirk said, "I'm feeling much more like my old self now—and it's time to get you off the hook. Christopher said you'd found something in that old despot's diary?"

"Yeah. Did you know his first name is Hercules?" sniggered Sooz.

Dirk raised an eyebrow. Hercules? What's wrong with that? he thought to himself.

Sooz continued, "And there's stuff about you in there—he thinks you're going to grow up to be a super-villain, you know, like Dr. Doom or something."

"Excellent!" said Dirk. "Maybe he isn't quite as much of a fool as we think he is. Little does he know I am already leagues ahead of Dr. Doom both in power and intellect! Although he does have a better suit of armor."

Dirk was about to launch into his trademark villain's laugh, when Sooz, recognizing what was coming, waved him into silence, saying, "But there's more. I read something about the school board wanting the receipts on the fireproofing that Grousammer should have done on the pavilion. Seemed a little odd to me. What do you think?"

Dirk was about to admonish her for interrupting a Dark Lord, when her words began to sink in.

"Of course!" said Dirk. "The pavilion wasn't fireproofed. That explains why it went up so quickly. And it was Grousammer's job to get it done. With money from the school budget, no doubt! Ha—I bet the wily old cur kept the fireproofing money for himself. It makes perfect sense—a classic cheap little greedy scheme to make a few extra gold pieces, typical of a second-rate tyrant like him. You wouldn't catch me coming up with something so petty! Oh no, by the Nether Gods."

"Shut up!" hissed Sooz suddenly.

Dirk scowled—that was the second time she'd interrupted him.

"Look, my mom!" She pointed down the road where a car was coming around the corner. "She's back from the store—you'd better go. I've been grounded, and I'm not supposed to see any of my friends for a week. Especially you." With that she shooed him away with her hands.

Dirk frowned in irritation. If only he could simply have Sooz's mom imprisoned by Orcs for being an inconvenient parent.

Sooz hurriedly retreated indoors. "I'll be back to school next week. See you then, Dirk."

"Don't worry, Nightwalker, I am going to sort

This is what I call a few extra
GOLD pieces, GROUSAMMER, YOU FOOL!

things out tonight. And with the information you have given me, Grousammer won't be asking any questions about it either!"

Sooz gave him a big smile at that, and then shut the door. Dirk hurried away.

He headed straight home, rushed indoors, and burst into Chris's room without even knocking. Chris looked up from the book he was reading in surprise. Dirk's face was lit up with a kind of unholy glee.

"Christopher! It's all real. I *am* the Dark Lord!" said Dirk excitedly.

Chris looked at him, bemused. "What are you talking about?" he said. "And you ought to knock before bursting in like that."

"*Bah*, a superior being like me need not follow the petty rules of your world. Listen, I burned my Cloak, and it opened a window onto my world. A window I could not pass through, unfortunately, but a window through which I could see into the Darklands. I saw Gargon, and my Iron Tower. Hasdruban's swine had . . . Well, anyway, I saw it!"

Chris stared at him, half horrified that Dirk might have cracked up completely, and half overjoyed that the old Dirk might be back.

Dirk ranted on. "The important thing is that if a window can be opened, then so can a door. But in the meantime, I want my friend Sooz back . . . Er, what I mean is that she is far too useful to be taken out of my service. It is time to come up with a plan to reinstate her, and get her name cleared. We shall call the plan the Wrath of the Goths."

"Are you going to tell them the truth, then? That it was you and not her?" asked Chris hopefully.

"What? No, of course not. I am the Great Dirk—I am never 'caught,' I never admit defeat, and I never 'take the rap'!" declaimed Dirk.

"I see," said Christopher icily. "So how are you going to get her off without turning yourself in? Or is your 'plan' just to let Sooz take the blame, let her be punished instead of you?"

"By the Nine Netherworlds, no. Of course not. We're going to rescue her, Christopher. Save her. Turn the tables—get her off the hook, as you mortals say. They cannot defeat me. And they will not crush my people either."

Christopher had to grin at that. "So what's next?"

"I am going to rebuild the pavilion, exactly as it was," said Dirk.

Christopher just stared at him for a moment. "Riiighht . . . ," he said.

Dirk looked over at him. "You don't believe me, eh? Well, wait and see. I'll see you later—don't wait up for me!" With that he spun on his heel and ran for the door.

Mike Acheson, the parking attendant, sat staring at the black oil slick that nestled near the pavement of what he called "The Cursed Parking Spot of Doom." No one ever parked there, or hardly ever. And if they did, something bad always happened. It was weird.

He could have sworn the oil slick had moved somehow. Maybe even gotten bigger. He stared at it some more. It fascinated him, as if it was calling to him, even mocking him.

He'd tried cleaning up the slick with a cloth. But the cloth dissolved in his hands. He'd tried hosing it away with water. No effect. He tried scooping it up with a shovel and putting it in a bucket but the stuff just slid off everything he tried to pick it up with. He'd tried setting it on fire. It wouldn't burn. Except your skin. It really burned if it touched your skin. Vile stuff whatever it was. Maybe he should get someone else in—Environmental Protection Agency or something. But that would be silly. It's just engine oil right? That's all. Engine oil.

The Rebirth

The next morning, Dirk rose extra early—he wanted to get the best view at the ball field. And he was rewarded. As the teachers and children arrived at school, they couldn't help but notice the new pavilion. And soon they all came streaming over to gawk in staggered amazement at the extraordinary sight before their eyes.

For there it was. The Players Pavilion. Standing there. Virtually identical to the old pavilion, down to the same patterns of weathering on the old wooden walls and on the doors. Even the posters and photographs of old sports teams, coaches, and stars that people had thought burned up in the fire were back on the walls inside. And the equipment—bats, balls, pads, and the like. It was as if the pavilion had never burned down at all.

The crowd began to grow in size. There were a few

gasps of amazement and shock, but mostly the gathering of children and teachers stood in awed silence. They simply could not believe what they were seeing. Soon cell phones came out and phone calls were made. It wasn't long before most of the children's parents were also on the scene.

Dirk overheard one of the teachers—old Grotty Grout the social studies teacher—say, "I thought there'd been a fire. Was I dreaming?"

The teacher beside him, Mrs. Batelakes, just turned to him and shrugged. "That's what I thought too—but perhaps we got the wrong story or something."

"Can it be real?" asked Grout.

"Well, yes. It appears to be, doesn't it? I guess someone made a mistake, and the place never burned down at all," ventured Battleaxe, running her hands through her hair as if she couldn't believe what she was seeing. Which was pretty much the case.

"I guess you're right—but I could have sworn I saw lots of smoke. Burned out ruins even. How peculiar. I mean, it looks just the same as the old one. Most odd," said Grout.

Dirk grinned triumphantly at this exchange and he gave vent to a great "*Mwah, ha, ha!*," with his fingers cradled together like a comic-book supervillain. The teachers turned to look at him. At the sight of Dirk laughing his evil laugh their eyes narrowed in suspicion. Dirk could almost hear them thinking, "Could this strange little boy have something to do with this? Surely not!" That made him feel even more triumphant. What a glorious day this was turning out to be!

Still grinning from ear to ear, he wandered off in search of Christopher and Sooz. He found them nearby, staring up at the new pavilion, their jaws agape.

"Is it the old pavilion somehow brought back from the past? Or regenerated? Or an exact copy?" Sooz was saying. "What's going on?"

"I don't know," said Chris, "but it's very strange."

Dirk nudged his friends, trying to get their attention. They didn't even notice. Dirk snapped his fingers in front of both their faces—finally they turned to look at him, amazed wonder in their eyes.

Dirk grinned. "It's not quite an exact replica of the old pavilion—look up there, right at the top where the clock is. See? Just under it," Dirk said, pointing upward.

They squinted for a closer look. They could just make out a small plaque with a strange pattern on it.

"It's my seal. The Seal of the Dark Lord—same as the one on my Ring!" said Dirk with pride. "I've left it there as a mark to show that I rebuilt the pavilion!"

"You . . . you did this?" said Sooz in amazement. A hand went up to her forehead. "Of course, who else could it be?" she added.

"Yes, it was me. I did it for you, Sooz—you're off the hook now, don't you see? How can they blame you for something that a court of law would have to say never happened? She burned down the pavilion, did she? But there it is, bold as brass, and very, very unburned! Brilliant, eh?"

"But . . . but . . . how?" said Christopher.

"Skirrits," said Dirk happily, as if that explained everything.

"Skirrits?" said Sooz in a puzzled tone.

"Yes, Skirrits. Little interdimensional beings that travel between the worlds. Something like Goblins or Spriggans or something, but more . . . well, intelligent, I guess. I . . ."

Dirk thought for a moment. Oh, why not embellish things a bit? Puff himself up?

"I summoned the King of the Skirrits to me with a mighty spell, and, in return for certain . . . er, pledges . . . I commanded him to rebuild the pavilion for me. So he sent forth one thousand and one Skirrits to earth, and they rebuilt the pavilion. Overnight. With magic and stuff." Dirk said this very casually as if this sort of thing was an everyday event for him. Which of course it was, in a way. Or used to be.

"Wow," said Sooz. "And you did all this for me?"

"Well, yes," said Dirk. "I got you *into* trouble, and now I've got you *out* of trouble."

Sooz smiled joyfully and jumped up and down on the spot, clapping her hands together with glee.

Dirk smiled at her indulgently, pleased in his heart

to see her so happy. Which was an odd feeling for him, but he just couldn't help himself. Then Sooz rushed over to give Dirk another big hug.

"By the Nether Gods, desist!" said Dirk, embarrassed by such a show. Then, to make matters worse, she kissed him on the cheek.

Dirk flushed bright red, feeling flustered and embarrassed, unsure as to what to do, so he just sort of sputtered for a bit. "Er . . . ah . . . I . . . umm . . ." That kind of thing. Which made Sooz giggle. But it made Christopher scowl.

"Right, so you expect us to believe you summoned a bunch of creatures from another world and they built a new Players Pavilion for you?" he said angrily.

"Well, yes," said Dirk, actually relieved to have something to do other than deal with the kiss. "That's what happened. I mean—look, there's the proof," he continued, waving at the pavilion like a Roman emperor waving at a triumphal arch he'd just built to celebrate his victories.

Chris frowned. He had to admit Dirk had a point. Still, he wasn't buying it.

"Yeah, but Skirrits? Magical beings from another world? More like construction workers or something," Chris said forcefully.

"Workers—construction or otherwise—what, overnight? And how would I pay these workers, anyway?" said Dirk, laughing.

"I don't know," said Chris angrily. "But there has to be some rational explanation that doesn't involve little magic Goblins from another dimension!"

Just then, Principal Grousammer, who had been gaping up at the pavilion in astonishment along with everybody else, noticed them chatting. He strode over rapidly and scowled at them.

"Susan Black! What is the meaning of this?" he snapped. "I was there—I saw the blasted thing go up in flames; I felt the heat on my face. What's going on? What have you done . . ."

Before Grousammer could go on any further, Dirk interrupted him and said, "Best not to ask too many questions, sir. All you need to know is that this one has been fireproofed. Properly."

At those words Grousammer's face went pale, as white as chalk. He stared at Dirk in horror, pulling at his beard manically.

"How . . . how . . . ," he stuttered.

"How do I know about the fireproofing, eh, Principal Grousammer? Well, I don't think you really want to know, do you? Let's just say we should both keep things to ourselves, hmm? Let sleeping dogs lie and all that?"

Grousammer blinked at Dirk in shocked surprise for a moment. Then he took a few steps back, as if trying to get away. His face was a mask of disbelief.

"Well, umm. Well, no matter then," he stuttered. "Er, all's well that end's well, and that sort of thing . . . ," he said.

"So, I can come back to school?" said Sooz, grinning.

"Why yes, of course, Miss Black. Everything's fine, just as if nothing had ever happened," said the principal before turning tail and striding off as fast as he could.

Sooz and Christopher giggled. Dirk smiled. Petty tyrants like Grousammer always crumbled when the going got tough. There was nothing they could do to Sooz now. And Grousammer wasn't going to ask any questions, that was for sure!

~~June~~ MISERY 7
I have drawn a picture of the Skirrits rebuilding the pavilion for me. Interesting little creatures, and very useful. Though I am slightly concerned about the price of their aid. One day it will come back to haunt me, I'm sure of it. I wonder what the Skirrit King will ask for?

PESKY LiTTLE SKiRRiTS At WORK

A Night Visit

It was late, very late. Christopher had gotten up to go to the bathroom and was on his way back to his bedroom when he heard a whimpering sound coming from Dirk's room. It was something he'd never heard from Dirk before, so he decided to investigate. He crept silently into Dirk's room. Dirk was lying in bed, asleep. But he was making strange moaning noises, as if he was terrified. He began to toss and turn, thrashing around, and his face was as white as the sheets covering him. Beads of sweat formed on his brow. It was obvious he was having some kind of really horrible nightmare.

Suddenly he sat up with a cry of terror and his eyes flew open.

"Oh, hello, Christopher," he said, as if he wasn't at all surprised to see him sitting by his bed at one o'clock in the morning.

"I've been having these terrible nightmares. Ever

since I fell into your curious little world," he continued, wiping the sweat from his face.

"I get nightmares sometimes too," said Chris. "Most people do, it's quite normal for humans, you know."

"Well, yes," said Dirk. "At first I thought that's all it was—a nightmare of some kind. But the Skirrit King set me right on that. As a traveler between the many Planes of Existence, he is often aware of others who also travel through different dimensions. He told me that Hasdruban—may the Curse of the Withered Plums shrivel up his parts—had wrought another great spell, and sent something after me."

Chris raised an eyebrow. The whole Skirrit thing was something he still wasn't really sure about, something he couldn't really believe. Not to mention the fact that Dirk had really gotten Sooz into trouble. Okay, he'd saved her, but still . . . And Christopher couldn't help feeling, well, a little jealous. Sooz had forgiven Dirk for it all so quickly. In fact, she seemed to like Dirk more than ever.

Christopher tried to speak, but Dirk interrupted him. "That meddling Wizard sent the White Beast of Retribution across the planes to finish me off. This isn't some dream I've been having—it is real! The Beast has been pursuing me psychically—in my mind, in my dreams, I mean—ever since I came here. And once it's found me in the Land of Dreams it will be able to find my body in the real world. And then it will eat my Black Heart, for its only purpose is to consume my Evil Essence, thus destroying me forever!"

Christopher squinted. Dirk was telling one of his stories again. This time more bizarre and outlandish than ever. And it was starting to get to him. Half of him believed it, the other half wanted to run out of the room screaming at the top of his lungs.

Dirk went on. "You know the White Lynx of Wendle they've been talking about in the papers? Well, it isn't a lynx. It's the White Beast of Retribution, a creature that sometimes appears in the real world, and the rest of the time inhabits the world of dreams, the world of the mind. Here, look! I drew it from memory," said Dirk. He reached under his pillow and handed a drawing to Chris.

Chris looked at the drawing in horror. It was terrifying! "Look, Dirk," he began, but Dirk wasn't listening. He went on, oblivious.

"I think I know how to defeat it, Chris, but I need your help. The only way it will ever cease to hunt is after it has eaten of the Evil Essence of its target. So that's what we have to do, you see!"

"Wait a minute, are you saying that the only way to defeat this thing is to be eaten by it? That doesn't sound good," said Chris, finally able to get a word in.

"Well, of course, yes, you're right," replied Dirk.

NOOOOOO, not thAt. Anything But thAt!

"But there is something I'd forgotten. You know the cursed parking rumor that went around school, about the spot in the Savemart parking lot that's always empty with the black oil slick no one can get rid of? Well, that's where I landed when I fell to earth. I was coughing pretty badly at the time—I remember I coughed up a blob of black mucus. That's what people think of as the black oil slick. It's not surprising they can't get rid of it—it is after all a blob of the Evil Essence of a Dark Lord. Not that easy to remove, I can tell you!"

"Right, I see," said Chris, though privately he thought this was really way out there, even more than Dirk's usual crazy Dark Lord stuff.

"So what we do," Dirk continued, "is that we go out and call the White Beast. I can make myself known to it, let it find me in my dreams, and then it will come to the parking lot, where we'll be waiting for it. Once it finds the black mucus, it won't be able to control itself and it'll have to lap up the black stuff. It'll have to! That's what it exists for. It must, because the black stuff is pure Essence of Evil, more powerful and alluring to the White Beast than the actual me, clothed as my Essence is in this puny human child's body. And once it's done that, it'll phase back to its own plane, its mission accomplished—or so it will think, and we'll have gotten rid of it once and for all."

Dirk looked up at Chris triumphantly, as if he'd just

come up with the most worked out plan since Hitler's invasion of Russia. And to be fair to Dirk, he had once written an essay on exactly that—ripping Hitler's plan to bits and pointing out how much better Dirk could have done it.

"All very good, Dirk," Chris said. "But what do you need me for?"

"Ah well, to protect me. You see, I'll have to be asleep to get the Beast to find me in my dreams. So there'll be a few moments when I'm vulnerable, before I can wake up. You can get in between it and me when it manifests in the real world," he said.

Christopher snorted with derisory laughter, "Oh yeah! You want me to get ripped to pieces while you hang out in the Savemart parking lot, is that it?"

"Oh no, my friend, not at all!" said Dirk. "It will be perfectly safe for you. The White Beast will have to bow down before you, like the Unicorn before the Virgin Maid. For you are of Pure Heart, and if one of Pure Heart stands at the side of the victim of the White Beast of Retribution, then the White Beast must be at peace. It cannot attack. Because if you stand by me, out of friendship or love, then Retribution cannot be visited upon me, because I must be worthy of Redemption! Do you see?"

Chris stared at him. "Pure heart? Me? Are you sure you're not just a bit confused because my surname happens to have the word 'pure' in it?"

"No, not at all," said Dirk emphatically. "Though it can't do any harm."

Chris's brow furrowed. The trust that Dirk had in Christopher's friendship kind of made him feel a bit guilty. Dirk really did see him as a friend. One of the very few friends he had. Just him and Sooz in fact. And maybe Sal. Chris sighed. He felt sorry for Dirk.

Dirk didn't even notice. He went on. "It's all nonsense of course—Retribution, Pure Hearts, Redemption, Forgiveness! *Bah*, what garbage! But these goody-two-shoes types, the Hasdrubans and the Paladins, they have to have their rules, you see, and they always insist on playing by them, oh yes indeed. Can't be a goody-goody if you don't stick to the rules. Which has always been their greatest weakness, of course. Hasdruban will be defeated by his own ridiculous code. Brilliant!" Dirk muttered on like this for a while longer.

Christopher just stood up, shook his head in disbelief, and went back to his own room. As he lay in his bed, he began to think. Dirk was back, that was for sure, and acting stranger than ever. But what if a lynx *had* escaped from a zoo or something, and there was one in the area? Lynxes weren't particularly big and were usually scared of humans, but still—what if they actually found the real thing? Chris wasn't going to protect him from a real lynx, for goodness' sake! Well, for evil's sake, Christopher thought to himself with a smile.

But the chances were that they'd never find the White Lynx of Wendle, and especially not by calling for it in the Savemart parking lot, so Chris didn't really have anything to worry about, did he? Unless of course, it really was the White Beast of Retribution, sent from another world to eat the Black Heart of Dirk. But that couldn't be true now, could it? Surely not!

The White Beast

It was Sunday night. Midnight. Dirk opened Chris's bedroom door as silently as he could. Chris was up, waiting for him, dressed in a black shirt and pants. He grinned at Dirk conspiratorially.

"I'm ready," whispered Chris. Dirk nodded grimly. Together they crept down the stairs and out of the house without waking the Purejoies. Dirk had been planning their little expedition for several days now. To Chris, it was a midnight jaunt, a bit of rebellion. To Dirk, it was a deadly game of cat and mouse. And he was the mouse. He could be destroyed forever, this very night. Unless he turned the tables. Could the hunted become the hunter?

"We shall see!" he said out loud.

"What did you say?" said Christopher.

"Oh, nothing, nothing. Let's go," replied Dirk.

They set off toward Savemart. After a twenty-minute

walk, during which they tried to avoid being seen—two young boys out on the town after midnight might attract some unwanted attention, especially from the police—they came to the Savemart parking lot. It was utterly deserted at this time of night—which was what they were hoping for, of course. Bright light from the main store kept the parking lot fairly well lit, but at the outer edges the light faded into a kind of shadowy twi-light. It was here, at the fringes of the parking lot, that Dirk had fallen to earth, all those months ago.

Dirk flicked on a flashlight. He would have preferred to use the Finger Flame Cantrip or the more powerful Orb of Illumination—magic spells didn't have batteries, and only ran out when you wanted them to. Still, human technology wasn't so bad.

He searched the parking spots, looking for one with a puddle of black oil. And there it was, the light glinting strangely from its slimy surface. Essence of Evil. Essence of a Dark Lord. Essence of Dirk.

Chris stared at it in fascination. He could almost feel it. As if it were calling to him, tempting him. Per-suading him to do things. Bad things. Evil things. He stepped back in trepidation. It must be a trick of the night, his mind playing tricks on him in this dark and deserted place. It couldn't actually be a puddle of pure evil, could it?

Then a thought struck him, and he said, "If it is

your Evil Essence, Dirk, why don't you take it back? Don't you miss it? All that evil?"

Dirk turned and stared at Chris, his face a pallid white mask in the dim light. A look of distaste seemed to cross his features.

"I thought of that . . . But somehow . . . it just felt . . . I didn't want . . ." Dirk's voice trailed off as if he couldn't finish what he wanted to say. Perhaps he didn't know what he wanted to say.

Chris continued to stare at the black slime. Somehow it drew him. "Maybe you'd get your old body back—you know, with the claws, and the horns and everything," said Chris absentmindedly. "And your evil laugh is sounding more evil these days . . ."

Dirk glanced over at him and frowned. He didn't like the expression on Chris's face.

"Step away from the Evil Essence, Chris," Dirk shouted. "That stuff can snare your soul! Even I dare not risk getting too close!"

Chris ignored him, so Dirk took him by the arm and led him away, making sure his back was to the slick black mucus.

"And anyway, I have thought about that too, but what do you think they'd do if I turned up at school with yellow tusks, massive horns, skull and bone showing all over the place and standing twelve feet tall? They'd probably call the SWAT team in or something!"

Chris seemed to snap out of whatever trance he'd been falling under, and laughed out loud.

"Ha, Mousehammer would try and put you in detention," said Chris.

"*Bah*, I wouldn't even fit in the detention room," said Dirk, looking over at Chris to make sure he was okay. He'd forgotten just how dangerous Essence of Evil was for humans.

"Anyway, Chris, I want you to stand here. Don't look at the black stuff, okay? I'm going to sit down nearby and try to doze off for a bit. When I'm dreaming, I'll let the White Beast find me."

"Then what happens?" said Chris.

"It should materialize nearby," said Dirk.

"What do you mean exactly by 'materialize'?" asked Chris.

"Literally appear out of thin air! I'll still be asleep—it'll try and come for me. You've got to get in its way—appease the savage Beast and all that. And if I don't wake up, you've got to wake me. Any way you can—shout at me, scream at me—by the Nine Netherworlds, kick me if you have to! Okay? Got it?" said Dirk, looking at Chris desperately.

"Yeah, yeah," said Chris dismissively. Chris didn't really believe anything would happen. There probably wasn't even a lynx on the loose as it was almost certainly a hoax—and he certainly didn't believe one of them was stalking through Dirk's dreams, trying to hunt him down inside his head. Chris sighed. Sure, it was fun sneaking out at night, but now the excitement was beginning to wear off. Here they were in some stupid parking lot, and what was he doing? Standing by while Dirk went to sleep. Oh, what fun . . .

Dirk shook Chris aggressively. "Listen, Chris, stop daydreaming! This is serious! The White Beast could kill me. Forever! Do you understand?"

Chris rolled his eyes. "Yes, yes, it will 'devour your soul' and 'consume you utterly for all time' just like you said the other night. No coming back as the undead. Not even as a mindless zombie. Gone forever, finito, kaput, bye-bye Dark Lord forever; yes, I get it, Dirk!"

"Okay then," said Dirk, eyeing Chris with worried concern. It was clear Chris really didn't get it. But once the Beast turned up, he would—pretty quickly. And Dirk had no real choice—it was only a matter of time before the Beast hunted him down anyway, and the chances were that it would happen when he was on his own and vulnerable. Asleep in his bed probably. No, better to have the thing find him on his own terms, on ground of his own choosing.

Dirk hunkered down, the black slick of Evil Essence just in front of him. He crossed his legs, Buddha style, and closed his eyes. After a few minutes he sank into a kind of trancelike sleep.

Chris glanced over at him. Dirk's eyes were shut. In the shadowy twilight his face was as pale as the moon. Then his eyes began to twitch. Suddenly his mouth curled up into a rictus grin of fear. His mouth gaped and he screamed out loud, a horrifying wail of sheer terror!

The hairs rose on the back of Chris's neck. Whatever was going on in Dirk's mind it was definitely frightening the life out of him. And Christopher too!

Then Chris took an involuntary step back. His heart started hammering in his chest, and his mouth suddenly dried up like desert sand. Something had appeared in the air. A little white ball of glowing energy. A strange scent filled the air—like burning gasoline and roses mixed together.

Chris took another step back. He couldn't believe what he was seeing—the white ball of energy was growing larger and larger! It was turning into some kind of brightly glowing, gigantic cat—a tiger perhaps, or a panther, or some kind of otherworldly leopard—much larger and more frightening than a lynx! It was glowing white like a photo negative—just like Dirk's drawing. Its jaws dripped with saliva, its teeth were long and savage, its talons sharp and deadly. Its eyes were forming into yellow globes of relentless hunger.

It was all Chris could do not to pee in his pants at the sight of it. It was utterly, utterly terrifying. Bad enough if it'd been just a real panther, but to see it come out of the air like that! A phantom leopard, a ghost tiger. It was too much! Chris turned to run for his life, a scream of fear on his lips. But as he turned he caught sight of Dirk, just sitting there asleep. And the White Beast? It was appearing a few feet *behind* him. Nowhere near the black mucus! Dirk would be completely at its mercy. With one bound it could be upon him. And it would rip off his head in the blink of an eye.

Chris panicked—he wanted so much to run. But he couldn't leave his friend in the lurch. For a moment loyalty and terror warred for control of his soul. Loyalty won. With a whimper of fear, he turned and ran back. Just as the White Beast was preparing to leap, Chris stepped over Dirk's sleeping form and ran right at the creature, blocking its way. He shouted at the top of his voice, "Dirk, wake up, Dirk! Dirk!"

The Beast bared its hideous fangs and roared. It raised one taloned paw, ready to rip Chris's head off with a single strike. Chris quailed back in fear but stood his ground, praying that Dirk had been telling the truth.

The Beast hesitated for a moment, paw raised to strike. It fixed Chris with a deadly stare.

It felt to Chris like it was looking into his very heart, into the deepest reaches of his soul. And then its ears went back and it sank back on its haunches. It lowered its head submissively. Then it rested its head on its paws gazing up at Chris passively. Chris couldn't believe it. Now it looked like nothing more than an oversized house cat, a big, white, shining Garfield. Chris chuckled. He even reached down and stroked the thing between the ears.

He looked around—Dirk was waking up slowly, as if from an anesthetic.

But then Chris's eyes were drawn inexorably to the black mucus. Dirk faded away from his consciousness, receding into the distance like a forgotten memory. Christopher's vision was overwhelmed with the sight of the glistening black slime. It filled his mind.

Strange thoughts began to race around Christopher's brain. What was he doing? All he had to do was step aside, unleash the White Beast. That would be the end for Dirk! No more competition for his parents' love. Sooz would be devastated, of course. And he could console her! She'd be his friend. She'd love *him*, not Dirk. Yes, this was his chance, his chance to finally be rid of that interloper, that cuckoo boy, Dirk Lloyd the usurper!

Without another thought, Chris acted. He stepped aside and backed off. "Go on, get him, Beast, get him," he heard himself saying maliciously.

The Beast jumped up and roared. Dirk woke up. He rose and turned.

"Christopher, why?" was all he could say before the White Beast leaped into the air and came crashing down on top of Dirk.

"By all that is unholy, noooo!" Dirk cried as the Beast's

slavering jaws slammed down at his throat, trying to rip it out with one bite. At the last moment, Dirk managed to get his left arm up, and the Beast's jaws closed around it.

Seeing this, Chris was shocked out of the evil miasma that had taken control of his mind. He screamed in horror. He dashed forward, trying to get in the way, trying to pull the thing off his friend, shouting, "I'm sorry, I'm sorry, I'm sorry," over and over again.

Dirk was gasping in pain—the Beast was biting down on his forearm. Through gritted teeth Dirk managed a few words—"Betrayal—heart no longer pure, nothing you can do. Back off, Chris, back off now!"

"No," said Chris. And he wrapped his arms around the Beast's neck, trying to pull it off. The Beast dragged Dirk backward, and then rose up, still gripping his arm, and shook itself, trying to get Chris off its back. The strength of the beast was enormous—Dirk, his left arm still held hard in its jaws, was shaken about like a rag doll, his face grimacing in a mask of pain. Chris was thrown through the air, to crash in a heap several feet away. He lay there, stunned.

But that gave Dirk time to come up with an idea. His eyes narrowed, his face took on a look of iron determination. He muttered a few words under his breath, and passed his free hand through the air in an arcane pattern. Suddenly his left forearm came away just below the elbow! The Beast couldn't believe it. For a moment it was confused, unsure. It had an arm in its mouth, but the arm was still moving! Dirk began to scramble backward along the ground. The hand in the Beast's mouth actually reached up and poked it in the eye. Despite the danger, Dirk managed a little snigger at that.

The Beast hissed and dropped the hand. Then it leaped after Dirk. But Dirk was on the other side of the black pool of mucus by now, and the Beast landed right in front of it. It stared at Dirk hungrily, readying itself for the final leap, but then its eyes dilated strangely, its mouth opened, and its tongue lolled. It made a strange sound, a greedy kind of mewling. Then it began to lap up the black slime like milk, purring as it did so. The dark slime coursed through its body filling in the negative whiteness with solid black lines, turning its strange otherworldly fur as black as coal. As its form took on the hue of shadows, it began to fade away, dissipating into the night like smoke in the wind. Soon all that was left were two glowing yellow eyes hanging in the darkness. Then they too faded out of existence. All was quiet.

Dirk lay back and gasped. His left hand crawled toward him. He picked up his Sinister Hand with his right one and reattached it to the stump, mumbling a few arcane spell words under his breath, his face screwed up in pain. White puncture wounds from the teeth of the Beast bled slowly from his arm. Considering the size of the Beast, they didn't look that bad. Nothing a few stitches couldn't fix.

Chris stood and watched all this in shocked horror

and amazement. For a start, it was obvious that everything Dirk had ever told him about—the Darklands, Skirrits, the spell of the Sinister Hand, Dark Lords and White Wizards, and all the rest of it—it was all true. That was hard enough to take in. On top of that, he felt an overwhelming sense of guilt for betraying his friend.

"I'm so sorry," he said. "Can you forgive me, Dirk? I don't know what came over me—it was like I was taken over or something. It wasn't . . ."

"There is nothing to forgive, Chris. I know what happened—it was the Essence of Evil. It took you over, made you do those things, spoke to the dark in your soul, corrupted you for a moment."

"Still, the White Beast nearly killed you because of me," said Chris, sorrowfully.

"And it could have killed you too. Easily. With one bite, with one swipe of its claw. But you jumped on its back, Chris, despite the risk. That gave me time to prepare and cast the Sinister Hand spell. That saved me."

"I . . . saved you?" said Chris.

"Yes! And anyway, it's all over now. A great weight has been lifted from my mind—I am free at last, free from the threat of utter destruction. The White Beast has been defeated. Hasdruban's plot has been thwarted! *Mwah, ha, ha!*"

Part Five:
Separation

ANOTHER CRAZY PLAN?

June ~~June~~ Misery 11
I have drawn up a map of my own world.
Hopefully soon I shall return to it and
take my place as its Dark Lord and rightful
ruler.

It was a few days later. Sal, Chris, and Sooz met up for lunch in the school playground as usual. Dirk and Chris had recovered from the incident with the White Beast. Well, Dirk had—though there would be permanent teeth marks on his left forearm, white scars burned into his skin from the bite of the Beast. But that was okay by Dirk. He was used to the scars of battle. Proud of them even.

It was different for Chris. He hadn't really come to terms with it. Sometimes he accepted things, which meant accepting everything—Dark Lords, White Wizards, Gargon, Orcs, Skirrits, pavilions, Sinister

Hands, spells and all the rest of it. But sometimes that was just too much to take in. When that happened, his rational mind took over and rejected it all. His mind tried to pass off the White Beast as some kind of hallucination or dream, so that things made sense again, so that it wasn't true that his best friend was like Sauron or Darth Vader, trapped in the body of a twelve-year-old boy.

But for now, Chris was coping well. It always helped when Sooz and Sal were around to lend a bit of reality to things. The four of them were chatting away just as they usually did.

"So, what's next, Your Dirkness?" said Sal.

"I must find another way to return to the Darklands," said Dirk. "It is my top priority. I must set things right there."

"Jeez—I hope it turns out better than last time. Not having a sports pavilion was a real pain even if it was only for a few days!" laughed Sal.

"Do not fear, Sports Lord Sal Malik," said Dirk regally. "I never make the same mistake twice, believe me."

"Have you had any ideas?" asked Sooz.

"No," said Dirk. He frowned, and put his head in his hands. "It's difficult. Very difficult."

"Well, what would you do if it was the other way around—say if you're in the Darklands and you want to get to earth?" asked Sal.

"Ah, now that I know where your earth is, and its planar position in the cosmos, the matter would be simple. I would cast the spell known as the Eclipse of the Gates of the World," said Dirk airily.

"So why don't you do that spell here then?" said Sal. "Other than that it wouldn't work of course, as there's no such thing as magic!"

"You may mock, but magic is real, believe me. Anyway, it's the ingredients. You can't get them on earth," said Dirk.

"Yeah? What do you need?" asked Chris.

"Well, you need the eggshell of a dragon, a witch's hand, the eyelashes of a Nightwalker, the beard of a tyrant, and an eclipse," said Dirk. "And there are no dragons, Vampires, or Witches on earth, a pity really."

"Hmm, I can see your problem," said Sal.

"Indeed. Though there is an eclipse of the sun in a month, as it happens," said Dirk.

"Oh yeah, I read about that," said Chris. Then he had a thought. "Actually, there is a dragon on earth. The Komodo dragon. It doesn't fly, but it's a huge lizard, with poisonous breath. Or saliva anyway. We did a thing on it in biology. Its saliva can kill a man in a week if not treated. You remember that display of reptile bones and eggs in the science lab? The eggs are from a Komodo dragon—donated by some ex-pupil of the school who became an explorer or something, years ago."

INGREDIENTS

"You know, Chris, you're right, by the Nether Gods! That would do. The Komodo—it'd make for a pretty respectable dragon back in the Darklands in fact, and not all dragons fly anyway."

"And there's that witches museum in Wendle—don't you remember? I took you there," said Sooz.

"Oh, yes, I'd forgotten," said Dirk. "But I don't recall a hand."

"That's because you didn't like the museum so you just trashed it. 'These aren't real witches' was what you said!" Sooz retorted.

"What's all this witch stuff?" said Sal.

"The Wendle Witches. They were a coven of witches—well, so it was said—back in the seventeenth century or something. They all got burned at the stake. One of their hands, mummified, charred—mostly a burned out husk now—is in the witches museum there. They weren't real witches of course, as Dirk kept telling me," she said, making a face at Dirk. "But they did get burned, which ought to make up for it, right? And people really believed they were witches," she continued.

Dirk thought for a moment. "Hmm. Indeed. That should make up for it, yes. The power of a hideous death—always excellent for magic spells."

"And Sooz is a Nightwalker, a Child of the Night, right?" said Chris.

"Yeah, you can have some of my eyelashes anytime, Dirk!" said Sooz, grinning.

"She's not a real Vampire, though," said Sal, laughing.

"How do you know?" scowled Sooz. "I might be. You never know."

"Yeah, right," said Sal. "Typical Goth!"

Dirk furrowed his brow and said, "Actually . . . she dresses like one. She thinks like one. She has posters of them up on her wall. I mean, what's the nearest thing to a Vampire on earth—a Goth, of course."

Dirk paused for a moment and added, "But Sal's right. She's not a real Nightwalker. There's no way around that."

"Actually," said Sooz, "remember that online game I like playing—the one you and Chris think is a cheapo version of *Battlecraft*, you know, the *Realm of Shadows*?"

"Yeah, cheapo knock-off," said Chris dismissively. "What about it?"

"Well, one of their character classes is a Nightwalker—a sort of Vampire-paladin type. I'm a twenty-sixth level Nightwalker in that. So technically I am a Nightwalker."

Dirk frowned again. And then he nodded. "*Realm of Shadows* is a bit . . . Er, how would you humans say it? Er, a bit lame, I guess. But still. Hmm, it might do. After all, you are the avatar of a Nightwalker in the *Realm of Shadows*, and I am an avatar of a Dark Lord here on earth. You know, it might just work! This is getting interesting."

Sooz smiled at that, and then made a face at Sal, as if to say, "See, Dirk thinks I'm a Vampire—or close enough!"

Sal just raised his eyes and groaned.

"And you keep saying Grousammer is a tyrant, right?" said Chris.

"Oh yes, we can all agree on that I think," said Dirk. Everybody nodded their heads vigorously in agreement.

"But how are you going to get his beard?" said Sooz.

Dirk thought for a moment. "Hmm, I think I might be able to find a way . . . Though just in case, you might have to give me an alibi, Sooz. If anyone asks—about anything actually—just say I was over at your house, playing *Realm of Shadows* or something. Actually, don't say that, say *Battlecraft*. I don't want anyone thinking I'm a *Realm of Shadows* player, do I? I have my reputation to consider," said Dirk.

Sooz shook her head in disgust. "It's a great game! You should try it," she said.

The conversation turned to a discussion of the merits of various computer games. Dirk announced that he wanted to make his own game—where the player is an alien being called the Dark One who'd crash landed his spaceship on earth. He has to enslave mankind using a combination of new technology and strange, interstellar magic.

"Why?" asked Chris.

"What do you mean?" said Dirk.

"You know, why does he have to enslave mankind?" said Sooz. "What's the point?"

"Well, you know . . . Er . . . Because . . . Well, because he just has to! What reason do you need?" said Dirk, puzzled by the question.

"You always need a reason," said Chris.

"Why? Conquest for its own sake—isn't that enough?" said Dirk. "And I want to call the game *Crush the Puny Humans Beneath Your All-Conquering Boot Heels.*"

"Oh come on, that's far too long a title for a computer game," said Sooz.

"What? How dare you criticize me? Anyway, why is it too long?" replied Dirk.

"Er . . . Because it's too long?" said Sal.

The conversation went on in this vein for some time, until lunchtime ended and they had to go back to class. As they walked back indoors, Grousammer was coming toward them down the corridor. Dirk came to an abrupt halt and began to stare at him avidly.

Grousammer looked back at the boy out of the corner of his eye, an uncomfortable expression on his face. As he drew near, Dirk stepped closer and held his hands up, as if taking the measure of his face and beard. Sooz and Chris expected some kind of violent reaction from the principal—at the very least a chewing out, if not a detention. But Grousammer just looked horrified at the sight of Dirk so close to him. So he accelerated past, hunching his shoulders oddly, as if expecting a knife in the back at any moment, muttering to himself as he rushed off down the corridor . . .

The Beard

Grousammer woke with a start. He was sitting up in bed, pillows heaped behind his back. That was odd—he didn't normally sleep like that. He could feel something scrabbling at his beard. Grousammer looked down . . . and his eyes widened in horrified surprise. There was a hand, a child's hand . . . *Someone else's hand!* And it was soaping his beard with a shaving brush. How extraordinarily bizarre! Was he still dreaming?

Grousammer reached over to swat the hand away, ready to leap up and call for help when suddenly he froze in terror. The hand . . . the hand . . . it . . . it *ended.* It ended in a kind of greenish, raw-red wound as if it had been recently severed at the elbow. There was only a forearm and nothing else. Yet it was still lathering away merrily as if nothing was wrong.

Grousammer was paralyzed with fear. He must be still dreaming. Was this some kind of bizarre nightmare brought on by the stress of that weird pavilion business and that strange, odd little child, Dirk Lloyd?

Then the hand carefully laid the shaving brush aside and reached for a straight razor that rested nearby in a bowl of warm water. Grousammer followed its movements with horrified fascination, still frozen in terror. Carefully, the disembodied hand began to shave him. Down one cheek, then the other. Then his upper lip. He could only stare at the ceiling in horror, as the hand gently tipped his chin back to shave his neck.

Grousammer's heart thundered in his chest, his body paralyzed by fear. Was this the end? Was the hand going to slit his throat? No, of course not. The whole thing was absurd—it couldn't be happening, it had to be a dream. So all he had to do was wake himself up. He closed his eyes and tried to force himself awake, but nothing happened. Then the shaving stopped and he looked down. The hand was carefully gathering the soaped hair of his beard and putting it all into a little plastic ziplock bag. Then, still holding the bag hooked over its thumb, the hand began to crawl away, hauling itself along by its fingers, like some kind of pallid white spider. It pulled itself up the curtain, and then out the open window of the bedroom.

Grousammer shuddered. It was over. The nightmare was over. He sank back into a kind of faint, and fell into a dreamless sleep.

The Wendle Herald

Local News

Mysterious Theft of Witch's Hand

Wendle's famous Witches Museum was the victim of a bizarre theft last night. In 1683, Anne Demdike, one of the Wendle witches, was burned at the stake. Her hand, mummified by the flames, was preserved in formaldehyde by the famous historian, philosopher, and brother of Demdike, Roger Bentham, shortly after her death. For centuries it was held by the Bentham family, until they donated it to the museum in 1973. It has been on display ever since.

Local detectives are baffled by the theft. "How much is a witch's hand worth?" said Detective Carwen Hughes. "Not much. So why steal one?"

The BLACK DIARY of DOOM:

The FINAL Entries

~~June~~ MISERY 13

Sooz gave me an eyelash today. I told her I needed at least ten of them, which she made a fuss about. Something about it making her sneeze every time she plucked one out, not to mention looking weird without enough lashes. Not my problem, I said, and she got all huffy. Almost refused to hand them over!

Then I had to clean off all the heavy black mascara they were covered in. I informed her that the next batch should be mascara-free, which seemed to annoy her even more!

I thought it a perfectly reasonable request. These mortals—I will never understand them.

~~June~~ MISERY 15

I saw the principal today. Nobody had
seen him for several days, but I wandered
by his office and found that his door
was ajar. I saw him at his desk—
holding a mirror up to his face and
feeling his recently shaven chin. His
face was a picture—pale, worn, and
haggard, as if he hadn't slept in days.
I couldn't help myself and burst out
laughing. He saw me then—and his face
went even paler! He just stood up shakily,
stepped over, and shut the door. By the
Nine Netherworlds, that felt good.

~~June~~ MISERY 17

Easy! After school today I broke into the
biology display cabinet and stole some
Komodo dragon eggshells. I didn't even
have to break any glass, and I doubt they
will even notice they are gone. By the
Nether Gods, I'm good! My plans are
coming together. Excellent! Mwah, ha, ha!

~~July~~ SOULS-OF-THE-DAMNED 1

Everything is ready for the Ceremony of
the Eclipse of the Gates of the World. The

mannequin is ready. The hand has been prepared. I have the Beard of a Tyrant and the eggshells of a Dragon. Sooz's eyelids have long since given up their lashes. Now it is only a question of waiting until the eclipse, on the third of July. Or Souls-of-the-Damned, as I shall call July from now on.

~~July~~ SOULS-OF-the-DAMNED 2

This will be my last night on earth. I am eager to return home, and do battle with that overzealous meddler, Hasdruban, and his Paladin fanatics. It will be a wonderful shock for the scheming old fool. But I will also miss the friends I have made here. Still, what must be must be. Perhaps one day I can return, or send for Christopher, Sal, and Sooz. In the Darklands, they will be great lords and ladies—I'll see to that!

The Eclipse

It was Souls-of-the-Damned 3, and it was a fine sunny day. The eclipse would begin at exactly 2:13 p.m. Dirk, Sooz, and Christopher stood on the baseball field just outside the old but new Players Pavilion. Sal was with his family, watching the eclipse in the park with a picnic.

"Does it really have to be done here?" asked Christopher.

"Yes, I'm afraid so. It's perfect—built by magical interplanar travelers, it is infused with just the right kind of sorcery," said Dirk nervously. He was excited, elated, expectant, but also worried and unsure. What if it didn't work this time? It *had* to work!

Dirk had built a small fire on the ground, though he hadn't lit it yet. On it he placed herbs and spices, similar to those he used last time, and another scroll sealed with wax.

"I must say, it seems like madness to use fire again!" said Sooz.

"Don't worry about it—we're outside this time, and anyway, the Skirrits fireproofed it properly. With a Fire Retardant Enchantment in fact—much better than the usual stuff," said Dirk.

"Ha, right. Well that's okay then," said Chris skeptically. But then he looked back at the pavilion. There it was, bold as brass, throwing his skepticism right back in his face. He almost wanted to try and set it on fire, just to see how fire-resistant it really was.

Sooz followed Christopher's gaze. She didn't really believe anything would happen, just like the last time. But there the pavilion was. Still, building a pavilion was one thing—it could be done without magic, couldn't it? Opening a portal between worlds, well, that was another thing entirely.

But Christopher had seen the White Beast, had seen the Sinister Hand in action. Sometimes he thought maybe he'd imagined all those things. But in his heart of hearts, he knew it was real. Either that, or he'd gone mad too, just like Dirk. Could madness be catching?

As if to prove that he really was mad, Dirk pulled out a small puppet from his pocket. It had been crudely fashioned from wood. Sooz's eyelashes had been stuck on where the eyes should be, and it was

FREAKY WOODEN puppet

wearing Grousammer's beard. It looked very unsettling indeed, like some kind of demon's toy doll.

"Jeez, that's freaky!" said Chris.

"Yeah, weird. Really weird. Can I have one, Dirk?" said Sooz, only half joking.

Dirk smiled, acknowledging her words, but not saying anything. He was deep in concentration. Next, he drew out the mummified witch's hand. He put the little mannequin doll into its palm and muttered something over it.

Sooz's and Chris's brows knitted in puzzlement simultaneously. Was it their imagination or did the hand tense up a little, as if it was gripping the doll? Surely not!

Then Dirk placed the hand and doll on top of the fire. He reached into his pocket and drew out a small box, covered in bloodred Glyphs. He flipped up the lid of the box. Inside were the Komodo dragon eggshells. They'd been crushed into a fine powder. He muttered some more unintelligible words, making arcane gestures over the box with his other hand.

Sooz and Chris looked at each other and tried not to laugh.

"All is ready," said Dirk. "Now we wait for the eclipse." He looked up at the sky, scanning the heavens for a sign. A few minutes passed. They stood in uneasy silence. Dirk's tense nervousness was rubbing off on Chris and Sooz.

"Time check, please," said Dirk tersely.

Chris checked his watch. "Er . . . ten past two," he said.

"It begins," said Dirk, and he raised his hands and began to chant. It was just like the last time—a strange, bizarre sound using words and phrases not meant for this world. Everything seemed to go quiet—birds stopped singing, the sounds of nearby traffic in Greenfield Lane seemed to fade. The hairs began to stand up on the back of Sooz's and Chris's necks . . . just like last time. They looked at each other nervously.

Dirk leaned down, still chanting, and lit the fire. It blazed up with a greenish haze. The hand seemed to react to the flames, tightening on the doll, squeezing it, crushing it. Was it their imagination, or could Chris and Sooz hear a kind of distant wailing as of someone howling in agony, someone that was being crushed to death, or burned alive?

Then the moon began to skulk across the face of the sun, and an answering shadow began to creep across the earth. The eclipse was upon them and an uncanny gloom was darkening the land.

Dirk suddenly stopped chanting and threw the powdered eggshells onto the fire. The flames flared up, greener, brighter, hungrier. Everything went silent as if the whole world was waiting for something to happen.

Then, without warning, black storm clouds began to gather with unnatural speed in the sky above Dirk.

Sooz and Chris glanced at each other, disbelief on their faces. How could this be happening? Surely it was just a coincidence? Or was it because Dirk really was a Dark Lord, and he was causing this with strange magic from another place and time?

Suddenly there was a crack of thunder, and a bright pool of red light began to form in the middle of the roiling thunderclouds. The sun was blotted out from the sky, and its wholesome light had been supplanted by a sickly ruby radiance, emanating from the bright crimson center of the black storm clouds in the sky, shining down on their small patch of earth like a celestial torch. Dirk threw his arms wide in welcome, his eyes closed in a kind of ecstasy. "Yes, yes," he cried. "Take me, take me!"

Chris stared in open-mouthed amazement. He could hardly believe this was happening.

He looked across at Sooz, to see how she was taking it.

Sooz, however, seemed to be in another state of mind entirely. She was grinning insanely, as if possessed. Her hair was beginning to stand up on end, crackling with energy, and her eyes seemed to glow red through the dark makeup over her pale skin, echoing the color of the sky. She was spreading her arms as well, and she was standing on her toes—or at least Chris assumed she was. It actually looked like she was floating a few inches off the ground!

Suddenly a lightning bolt of crimson energy lanced earthward from the center of the reddish glow. Dirk tensed expectantly, but then, incredibly, the bolt struck Sooz instead of him with a crackling blast of sound like a sonic boom! She gasped in shock and pain, and began to shudder and shake horribly. The red lightning didn't fade away or dissipate like normal lightning. In fact, it continued to crackle and burn, holding her in place, discharging vast amounts of power into her, like some kind of laser beam from the heavens, enveloping her completely. She began to smoke.

Dirk looked around confused. Why hadn't he been struck by the bolt? What was going on? Then he saw.

"Sooz!" Dirk cried in fear and distress. "No!"

Chris began to sprint toward her, shoulder first, intent on knocking her away, out of the ruby beam that held her transfixed, crucified by light. Crimson light burst out of her eyes and mouth and she fell backward. But she didn't fall to the ground. She began to float. Several feet off the ground. Then she began to scream. A horrible scream of agony and pain that pierced Chris's ears and heart like a punishment from God.

Chris sobbed in fear. As he got closer, he was struck by a wall of heat—in seconds his hair began to crackle and burn and his eyebrows were singed.

"No, Chris! No! There is nothing you can do," shouted Dirk. "The heat will kill you!"

And he was right. Chris couldn't get close, he had to back away—the heat was unbearable. Then a circle of darkness, blackest black against the reddish gloom, began to grow and spread around Sooz. It resolved itself into a kind of doorway, a portal into another world. An alien wind blew from that land to this, laden with strange smells and sounds, unfamiliar, unknown. Shapes began to form, to become more distinct. Chris could see a range of gray, barren hills, a desolate plain, and in the distance, a tall dark tower of peculiar design, reaching to the red-tinged sky of that foreign land like a claw reaching up to scratch out the eyes of heaven.

"The Darklands. She is being taken to the Darklands! How can this be?" howled Dirk.

Sooz was suddenly propelled through the opening. In an instant the crimson bolt clicked off, the thunderclouds faded away, and the dark opening narrowed to a point and snapped shut with a tiny popping sound. Sooz was gone.

The moon skulked on, and bright, wholesome sunlight began to brighten the earth once more. Chris couldn't believe it. How could this be happening? And was Sooz all right? Was she still alive? He turned to Dirk, with angry questions on his tongue.

Dirk looked upset. Incredibly, Chris could see tears in his eyes. He'd never seen Dirk cry before, never. That shook Chris, more than anything.

"Is she still alive?" Chris asked querulously.

Dirk wiped his eyes and pulled himself together. "Oh yes, yes, she's alive all right. The Crimson Bolt won't have harmed her, despite what it looked like. But she is in the Darklands. That's not the best place to be for a young girl, even a Goth."

"What are we going to do?" said Chris.

"Well, we must try and rescue her, of course," said Dirk. He stood there, his brow furrowed, turning the Ring on his finger around and around as he thought.

Dirk went on. "But I can't understand it. The Crimson Bolt should only strike the one who wears the Ring of Power. It shouldn't have gone for her at all."

Chris blanched. His face went as pale as the moon. "Oh no," he said, putting his hands over his mouth. "Oh no . . . ," he mumbled through his hands.

Dirk's brow furrowed. "What? What is it?"

Chris put his hands down. "The Ring. She *was* wearing the Ring! It's all my fault!"

"What do you mean?" said Dirk.

"You remember when you asked me to steal the Ring back from her? I didn't do it in the end," said Chris.

Dirk's jaw dropped in amazement.

Chris went on. "I just couldn't do that to her behind her back, I just couldn't. Not to a friend. So I told her you wanted it back. She said that you can't just take gifts back from people you give them to—and she's right, you know."

Dirk just stared at the ground. He growled in anger, though he couldn't deny the truth of what Chris had said.

Chris carried on. "She thought about it, but in the end she just couldn't bear to part with it. And she was pretty angry with you for trying to make her. So, we came up with a plan. We had a few days before she went swimming, so we had a jeweler make an exact copy of it and gave that one to you."

Ah, so that's why she didn't seem bothered about losing it, thought Dirk to himself.

Chris went on. "We didn't think it would make any difference—we thought it was just a ring. And that's why the Crimson Bolt went for her . . . And now she's in the Darklands!" Chris fell to his knees and wailed, "I didn't know! I didn't know the Ring was so important! Why didn't you tell me? And now Sooz is gone."

Dirk looked enraged for a moment as if he was ready to strike Chris with a terrible spell of Destruction. But then he sighed and the rage left him. He put a comforting hand on Chris's shoulder. "Don't blame yourself, Chris. You're right—I should have told you how important the Ring was to the Ceremony. But I didn't think. I should have guessed. But what can we do? What's done is done."

Dirk helped Chris to his feet. Together they began to walk slowly back home.

"We have to help her," said Chris.

"Of course," said Dirk. "We won't abandon her. I'll think of something, don't you worry. Together we'll save her!"

Chris began to feel a bit better. Dirk *was* a great wizard, after all. They'd find her, he was sure of it. Then a thought struck him.

"Dirk?"

"Yes, Chris?"

"That was your Iron Tower of Despair we saw, wasn't it?"

"Yes, Chris, yes, it was. Impressive, eh?"

"Yeah, but, umm, was it my imagination, or wasn't it, well, wasn't it actually *pink*?"

Dirk sighed. There was still so much to do.

The END

EPILOGUE:
SOOZ IN THE DARKLANDS

Slowly, oh so slowly, the distant tower atop the hill grew larger as Sooz slogged across the darkling plain. As she drew nearer, she could see it glowing pinkly in the reddish midday sun of the Darklands. She thought about how upset Dirk would be when he found out they'd painted his Iron Tower of Despair pink! If she'd been one of those "Normies" in her school, she'd love it to be pink and fluffy, maybe with a little pink ribbon around the top. But Sooz was a Goth—pink was hideous. Repainting it black, that would be the answer.

Suddenly a large dark shape rose up out of the shadows of a nearby tumbled pile of rock. Sooz stepped back in terror, and screamed. She was on her own, a little girl alone in the Darklands and before her stood what could only be some kind of hideous demon, at least seven feet tall, covered in scaly skin, with a horned head, talons, and fangs. A great leather belt at its waist seemed to have shrunken human heads hanging from it. The thing shrugged—from its shoulders great bat wings extended with a leathery snap. It leaned down and hissed at her—plumes of foul-smelling smoke spewed from bony nostrils. Sooz cowered back, falling to the ground, hand raised. She was just a kid! A girl lost in this terrible land! She wished Dirk were here to help her.

As she quailed, a look of triumph appeared in the red glowing eyes of the demon and it leaned closer and roared, bathing her in a truly awful wash of bad breath. She shivered and tried to crawl away. But then a thought struck her. The demonic figure looked familiar. She narrowed her eyes and stared. Then she got up, and stared some more, looking the strange thing up and down. This seemed to surprise the huge demon—an almost comical look of puzzlement framed its face. Little girls weren't supposed to do that.

Sooz said, almost to herself, "You look like the lead singer of that band Chris likes so much. What were they called? Morti—that was it."

On closer inspection the demon, if that's what it was, looked a bit raggedy around the edges. Half starved and filthy, as if it'd been on the run for months. The demon looked around, as if bemused. Little human girls were supposed to be terrified of him.

They weren't supposed to talk back, that was for sure. Then the girl took a step toward him. That really worried him. They certainly weren't supposed to walk up to him, fearless and confident! Suddenly she extended a hand and spoke.

"Hello. You must be Gargon. Dirk gave me this Ring." She held up her finger. The Ring was glowing with an unearthly light, an eerie dark light that bathed Sooz's face in a Vampiric glow, that gave her a ghostly beauty.

The demon's great fanged jaw dropped open, and a look of joy crossed its unholy features.

"It is the Great Ring! My Lord lives! My Lord lives," said Gargon, in a dark, gravelly demon's voice; for it was indeed him, Dirk's lieutenant, Dread Gargon, the Hewer of Limbs, Captain of the Legions of Dread.

"And he gave you his Great Ring! He has chosen you!" bellowed Gargon. He dropped to one knee.

"Gargon swears fealty to the Dark Mistress, Queen of the Night, and betrothed of my Lord! I will serve you in the name of the Dark Lord! I will be your faithful servant, my queen."

Sooz stood there for a moment. Then a little half smile lifted one side of her mouth. Fantastic! A seven foot demon. Her faithful servant. How cool was that! Now she wasn't so vulnerable, so weak, so alone. She had protection—not just any old protection either, but

protection from a seven foot winged and taloned . . .
er . . . thingy whatsit.

"Hey, I'm loving those bat wings, Gargon," she said.

"Thank you, my lady!"

ACKNOWLEDGMENTS

I, the Great Dirk, would like to claim this work entirely as my own, but I suppose I ought to thank my two worthless hirelings, those soon to be undead ghost writers, Jamie Thomson and Dave Morris, for their contributions. I would also like to condescendingly thank Gregor Smith McGregor of Clan McGregor of McGregor from the Island of the McGregors for his invaluable work in pointing out and correcting the absurd errors and mistakes perpetrated by the above mentioned undead fools, Thomson and Morris (note to self: must punish them). Also, Darren Cheal the Fishlord for his support as well as Detective Inspector Carrrrwen Hughes for his help in certain . . . errr . . . legal matters. And Katherine Haslem (called the Spider Queen) for more help with fixing the ghostly drivel of my undead writer-slaves. Oh, and my lackeys—sorry, I mean friends—Sooz, Chris, and Sal for allowing me to write about them. Actually, they didn't have any choice in the matter, but still, they deserve some recognition.

By the Nine Netherworlds, that tedious lickspittle Thomson insists that I also thank his brother, Peter, for his advice. Apparently, this brother is not actually undead, but I'm sure I can sort that out, given time.

By the Nether Gods! Will it ever end? Now that stinking piece of undead flesh known as Thomson is insisting I thank his partner, Lucy Alwyn, for all her support too! Ha, she has my sympathy also, the poor woman.

And finally, I must also thank Megan Larkin, my slave editor at the publishing house I have honored with my great work, Orchard Books. Thomson tells me she was very useful, and I am glad she survived the Nightgaunt I sent to her house. I think I overreacted a little when I read some of the corrective work she had done on the manuscript. I fear that Matt Ralphs, the second slave editor, did not though. This could be a problem for Book Two, as, in hindsight, he was also rather useful. No wait, I'll bring him back as a zombie too! There, decided.

The Author

Originally from a world beyond our own, Dirk Lloyd lives in the town of Whiteshields, where he spends most of his time trying to get out of school and back home to his Iron Tower in the Darklands.

He has been a Dark Lord for more than a thousand years. Some of his achievements include: building the Iron Tower of Despair; raising vast armies of Orcs and Goblins; waging great wars; destroying many cities; casting mighty spells and enchantments; and excelling in English, science, and math classes at school.

He has only recently turned to writing. Be warned—reviewers who adversely criticize this work will be hauled off to his Dungeons of Doom, subjected to the Racks of Pain, and then consigned to the Slave Pits of Never-Ending Toil for all eternity.

The Seal of Dirk

NEVER FEAR, DEVOTED
MINIONS, MY STORY
CONTINUES . . .

DARK LORD
SCHOOL'S OUT

Greetings,
puny humans—
get ready for
world domination!

JAMIE THOMSON
DIRK LLOYD

Aaaaaaaaaaaarrrrrrrrrggggggggghhhhhhh!" Her fall seemed to go on forever through an endless gulf of space. Then, suddenly—

Ker-splat!!!

Sooz lay on her back, exhausted, winded, staring up at a strange reddish sky . . . The last thing she remembered was Dirk's voice, hypnotically mumbling strange words as the moon's shadow crept across the face of the sun. And then . . . then a burning ruby agony and a feeling of falling, falling, as if in a dream.

She coughed and turned her head. She was lying in a kind of dirty-water-colored plain that stretched off into the distance. Her brow furrowed in puzzlement. The grass was the wrong shade of green. It was too dark and the sky had a reddish tinge to it. And . . . and . . . there were two moons! Two! One was a pale white, the other a diseased-looking red. How could that be?

A faint breeze blew up, ruffling her dyed black hair. Her nose wrinkled. The breeze had a strange tang to it, a scent she'd never smelled before. It was like a cross between the sea and cinnamon—a not unpleasant smell in fact, but strange, and because of that, rather disturbing.

This was all Dirk's fault. That weird, funny kid who'd turned up at school claiming to be a Dark Lord exiled from his own lands, which he called the Darklands. She and her friend Christopher hadn't really believed him, but they had played along—even helping Dirk try to get back to his homeland. The first time, they'd just ended up burning down the school sports pavilion (and she'd gotten blamed for it!). Then they'd tried again, with some kind of spell, but this time . . . What had happened this time?

Sooz sat up. Whatever the smell was, it wasn't the smell of her land. It was the smell of a strange land, a foreign land, a land unknown. It was the smell of the Darklands . . .

How on earth was she going to get home?

MeANwhiLe, BACK oN EARTh...

August SOULS-of-the-DOOMED 4

Ten thousand curses on the heads of fluffy little bunny rabbits! I cannot believe what has happened! The Ceremony of the Eclipse of the Gates of the World was supposed to send me back home, but it failed and Sooz has been exiled to the Darklands instead of me! How I fear for the safety of my little Child of the Night. No, wait . . . What I mean is that I hope my useful servant, Sooz, has not been damaged. That would be inconvenient.

August SOULS-of-the-DOOMED 5

Sooz has been reported missing. Her mom is very upset, as are quite a few people at school, in fact. I never knew Sooz was that popular.

The police interviewed me about it. They asked me all sorts of questions about Sooz, such as when I saw her last, what was she wearing (as if I could remember that—Goth stuff, what else?!), and other such petty questions that vex the minds of these puny humans. Anyway, as I am such an honest and upstanding citizen I told them the actual truth—that I had cast a mighty spell, and that it had gone wrong, resulting in Sooz being transported to another plane because she was wearing my Great Ring of Power and she was now in a place called the Darklands, which is very dangerous, full of Orcs and Goblins and ravening Eagle Riders and fanatical paladins. They didn't believe me of course. Anyway, apparently, now I have to see those feebleminded child psychos, Wings and Randle, again. What a bore!

I have kept a newspaper clipping about Sooz. She would be pleased to see her photo in the paper. Or perhaps "stoked." Yes, that's the word she would use. Stoked. How I miss her.

Dirk sat in his room, staring glumly out of the window at a cloudy summer sky, brow furrowed in angry thought. Next to him sat a young boy with bright blue eyes and corn-yellow hair, also staring at the darkening sky. The boy seemed to radiate a kind of innocent beauty. Dirk did not. It was as if an angel and a devil were sitting next to each other in quiet friendship.

Dirk heaved a sad sigh, full of frustration and despair.

"So, what are we going to do?" said the young boy.

"I don't know, Chris, I don't know," said Dirk in frustrated tones. He sighed again. "I can't think of anything. There is no way to get there without the Ring, and that's the end of it."

"But she could be in real danger. I mean really serious stuff. Not like getting an uber-detention for burning down the school pavilion or something, but real stuff, like getting chopped up by Orcs or . . . or . . . It's just so awful I can't bear thinking about it!" said Chris.

"If only I could just talk to her, then I could help, tell her what to do, tell her how to handle things in that dread land," Dirk said. "There are great opportunities there, if you know how to take advantage of them."

Chris lifted up his cell phone and gazed at it. "If only we could just call her. I've tried, but it just says, 'That person's phone has been turned off or is unavailable.'"

"Ha, well, it would, wouldn't it? She's not going to

Just Chillin'

get a signal in the Darklands! Well, not that kind of signal anyway."

Dirk's eyes narrowed and he began to stare at Chris's phone. A maniacal gleam appeared in his eyes. Always a bad sign, Chris thought to himself, the maniacal gleam. It meant Dirk was coming up with another crazy scheme.

"Not that kind of signal . . . ," Dirk muttered to himself. "Yes, of course!" Dirk yelled, and he leaped to his feet, snatching Chris's phone.

"All I have to do is modify this device—I'm sure I can get it to transmit the right kind of signal—or more accurately, open a magical doorway between the planes through which sound can travel. We can't travel ourselves, but sound can! Much easier."

"That's great, but why does it have to be my phone? Why don't you get your own?" said Chris, half-pleased they might be able to help Sooz, half-worried about Dirk's plans for his phone.

"*Bah*, I'm not getting a phone. Your parents—jailers, more like—would use it to track me constantly, as would the High Council of the White Shields, those witless lackeys of my archenemy, that old fool, Hasdruban, the White Wizard!"

"I don't think the local council works for the White Wizard, Dirk. Dark forces, yeah, according to Dad, but not the White Wizard. I mean, you're just being paranoid. And my mom certainly doesn't—she's a minister for goodness' sake!" Chris replied.

"All the more reason why she would be working for the White Wizard! Anyway, even if what you say is true, why take the risk? I'm a Dark Lord—I'm supposed to be paranoid. How do you think I've survived for this long?" said Dirk.

"Yeah, well, whatever, Dirk," said Chris. "The thing is, will I get my phone back?"

"That depends. If my plan works, probably not, no," said Dirk.

"Why, what are you going to do?" said Chris, worried.

"I'm going to reengineer it. Magically enhance it. I'm going to turn it into a DarkPhone."

"A DarkPhone? What's that?" said Chris, even more worried.

"Well, you know, an evil phone. A kind of Undead phone. But first of all I need a little sliver of bone, taken from the skeleton of someone bad, like a murderer or a thief, someone like that. Preferably someone who was hanged for their crimes. Even better, hanged at midnight at a crossroads on Halloween or May Day or something," said Dirk, as he removed the SIM card from Chris's phone.

"Riiiight . . . And where do you think we're going to find that?" said Chris, shaking his head.

"I'm not sure, but we must at least try," said Dirk, throwing the SIM card into the trash can.

"Hey, what are you doing?!" protested Chris loudly.

"You won't be needing that anymore, Christopher," said Dirk as he pocketed the phone. "From now on, this phone will run on magic. Necromantic magic. Well, as soon as we can find that piece of bone."

Christopher stared at Dirk in irritation. Dirk just grinned back at him. Chris gave an involuntary shudder. He'd known Dirk for some time now, but that grin still sent a shiver down his spine.

Christopher didn't really want to encourage any more of Dirk's crazy plans, but on the other hand he was ready to do whatever it took to bring his friend Sooz back. "Wait a minute . . . ," he said.

Dirk raised an eyebrow. "Don't imagine for a moment that I shall be returning your phone. It's been requisitioned for the war effort."

"No, no, I just had an idea."

"Really? What?" said Dirk.

"Swamp people," replied Chris.

"Swamp . . . what?" said Dirk, confused. "Has it come to this, that you now resort to hurling insults at me? It is I that should be handing out the insults, not you!"

"No, no. Swamp people. The remains of human sacrifices. Ritually sacrificed and then thrown into peat swamps thousands of years ago. Their bodies are amazingly preserved by the peaty mud. And they were sacrificed by being strangled and then having their throats cut. Really gruesome!" said Chris excitedly.

Dirk's face lit up at the thought of it. "That is perfect! Absolutely perfect! You are a genius, Christopher, a genius. Well, obviously not compared to me, but pretty good all the same. For a human child. Anyway, where can we find one of these?"

"There's one in the museum at Fetbury. Fetbury Man they call him," said Chris.

"Fetbury? Where's that?" asked Dirk. "And what a stupid name. You humans have such stupid names for places, you really do. Why can't you call it Deadbury or something? You know, where the dead are buried—and rise again to serve their evil necromantic masters—hopefully me. *Mwah, ha, ha!*"

"Deadbury. Right, okay. Well, Deadbury's not far. We could get a bus or a train there, no problem," said Chris.

"Excellent, we shall go this afternoon," said Dirk.

"We can't—Mom's church festival is later, and we have to go to that," said Chris.

"Nooooooo!" wailed Dirk.

ROCK CANDY
OF DOOM

By the Nine Netherworlds, they're covered in slime and mud like the filth of a thousand years!" said Dirk.

"What, swamp people you mean?" said Christopher.

"No, these vile human children! Look at them," said Dirk, gesturing imperiously with one hand.

Before them, in a large sandbox, several kids played. They were indeed dirty, faces smeared with chocolate, hair matted with pink cotton candy, clothes stained with soda—and worse.

Dirk and Christopher were standing behind a makeshift booth selling homemade jams, jellies, and juices. All made by Chris's mom, the Reverend Purejoie. Several other booths were scattered around the play area, selling similar goods. It was the church festival.

"*Bah*, I've said it before, and I'll say it again—they're like an unruly tribe of Goblins, all of them!" said Dirk.

"Actually, Goblins would be easier to control—an execution or two, and they'd soon be standing at attention!"

"You can't execute children!" said Chris.

"Why not?"

Chris just looked at him. Dirk raised his eyes and sighed. "No, I suppose not; a pity."

"Anyway," said Chris. "What if they could? You'd be first, probably!"

"Ha! Good point. Now, as the Mouth of Dirk and my closest counselor, what do you think our plan should be for the assault on the Dead and Buried Museum?"

"Assault? Come on Dirk, we can't attack the place! Anyway, who would do it, you and me? Armed with what? Pencils and notebooks?"

Dirk narrowed his eyes. Sarcasm? Was he being mocked? He was about to admonish Christopher when he noticed something big in the sky. A large balloon, floating serenely by, with a big basket full of humans hanging below it. He gazed up, fascinated, Christopher's disrespectful remark forgotten.

"What makes those float, Christopher?" he said.

"What?" said Chris, following Dirk's gaze upward. "Oh, hot air balloons. Helium gas, I think."

"Helium, huh?" said Dirk. "Interesting. Think of it, a few hundred of those, say, with a crew of Goblins—proper Goblins, not these puny human children. They could drop stuff—you know, like darts and bombs and stones. Make short work of Hasdruban's Paladins, wouldn't they! There are so many things I could do with earth technology, if I could only get home!"

"They're not easy to make though," said Chris.

"True, but a lot easier than one of your jet planes or tanks or whatever," said Dirk.

Just then, their neighbor, a kindly old lady called Mrs. Morris, walked past with a tray.

"Rock candy, delicious rock candy," she said.

"Rock candy! I love rock candy," said Chris, all plans to build Goblin-crewed hot air balloons or to raid the archaeological museum in Fetbury forgotten. "Do you want some, Dirk?"

Dirk frowned. "Rock candy? Why would I want to eat rock? Oh, wait, I get it! We use the rock candy as projectiles to smash a window in the museum and break in that way. Or better yet, as ammunition for our Goblin battle balloons! You are clever at times Chris, you really are."

Chris laughed, "No, no, you nitwit, they're not made of rock, they're just called that, they're—"

Dirk suddenly interrupted him. "Did you just call me a nitwit? What is this 'nitwit'?" he said forcefully, not sure whether to be angry or not.

Chris blinked. The last thing he needed was one of Dirk's tantrums.

"Umm . . . Er, a nitwit is like . . . It's like, er . . ."

Revenge is sweet!

Dirk narrowed his eyes once more. Chris was getting really disrespectful these days. If only he could cast one of his spells—that would set him right! Nothing too harsh, mind, but still, something to remind him who was boss. Maybe the Malediction of Unmoving Obesity. If only it worked on this plane . . .